Praise for *People and Peppers,
A Romance*

"*People and Peppers, A Romance*, draws on complex interactions between diverse peoples, men and women, from Dominican Republic, Trinidad, New York, and Japan. Kelvin Christopher James captures their intimacies and compromises with fluent, accurate, and tasty expression in an ecology of people and pepper varieties in the field, and with his sweet language, they linger on the reader's mental palate."

—Dr. Brader Braithwaite, Faculty of Medical Sciences University of the West Indies

"*That's jealousy for you,*" *pronounced Andaluza with a heavy sigh,* "*Child, lemme tell you something. Jealousy will kill you. One way or the other it is poison to yuh body and soul and it certainly will kill you.*"

Nikki put up a defensive hand. "*Don't put me in that ward, Mammy. That ent me at all . . .*"

"An exchange from *People and Peppers, A Romance*, a brief passage in this impressive and insightful depiction of a subtle Trinidadian culture. This is the narrative magic of Kelvin Christopher James's prose: a bit of dialogue that paints a picture, promotes a philosophy, and just plain old entertains.

"Put me in that ward of James's admirers!"

—Walt Taylor: Civil Engineer, Trini-man

"A delightful tale"

—Eric Darton

"Excellent! What a pleasant trip! Trinidad to New York and back for the time of this novel. After the excitements from reading the romance of Peoples & Peppers, I had to cool down with a coconut water with a splash of brandy—*a la* Ramiya, the Taino lady in the book . . . James has sealed his reputation of being a nifty and insightful storyteller . . . a rich and diverse collection of worlds, which, with his brilliant narrative, live and glow. His principle characters are complex, motivated, and fun . . . the story is driven by the schemes and dreams of Vivion K Pinheiro, a man living off the strings of privilege and luck . . . bottom line, this patently feminist novel successfully demonstrates women's sympathy and tolerance in the name of love.

"Hats off to Kelvin Christopher James for a tale very nicely told."

—G. Agudo, Director, A Literary Salon,
Yomama Arts, New York City

" . . . with sparkling prose that engages and absorbs, the reader is effortlessly transported into the intrigues and emotional spaces that people this lively, entertaining novel!"

—M. Fullerton, Director, The Buzz Limited
Advertising Agency

"Entertaining . . . Something desolate and dangerous lurks here, reeking of neglected gods that underlie this novel like blue veins under dark skin."

—*Los Angeles Times*

"*A Fling with a Demon Lover* is unlike any book I've read. It's part romance, part mystery, part strange magic, and part personal quest. The characters . . . become so compelling you cannot put the book down until you discover the secrets of their separate stories."

—Whitney Otto, author of
How to Make and American Quilt

Praise for Kelvin Christopher James'
Jumping Ship and Other Stories

"James's stories form a vivid and often searing exploration of Caribbean experience on the islands, in New York, and in between. He writes about voodoo, dope, sex, friendship, children and a host of other themes with unflagging energy and insight. He is a gifted writer with a salty imagination and a genuine understanding of the worlds he inhabits."

—Patrick McGrath, author of *Spider*

People and Peppers
A Romance

Kelvin Christopher James

Harvard Square Editions

New York

2015

People and Peppers, A Romance

Copyright © 2014 Kelvin Christopher James

None of the material contained herein may be
reproduced or stored without permission of the
author under International and Pan-American
Copyright Conventions.

ISBN 978-1-941861-98-1
Printed in the United States of America

Published in the United States by
Harvard Square Editions
www.harvardsquareeditions.org

In respectful memory of Dr. Julian Stanley Kenny,
Environmentalist who initiated ecology awareness in
Trinidad and Tobago, 1930 – 2011

To my children

ooOoo

The People

Eduardo Gaspar Pinheiro

PATERFAMILIAS EDUARDO GASPAR PINHEIRO was a forward-thinking Portuguese colonialist who ruled over a sugarcane plantation in Santo Domingo for a decade or so of the early twentieth century. A rum-drinking mustachioed sophisticate of noble heritage, an aficionado of art and music, he was a generous patron of the Church, and felt distinguished for having been an intimate of Granados, the heroic composer—the non-swimmer who drowned in an effort to save his foundering wife.

Señor Pinheiro was a modern man; a proud, successful fellow kept wealthy by the fortunes of his well-managed plantation.

Eduardo's wife, Sybil Katarina Pinheiro died of typhoid in the tenth year of their marriage, the ninth since she journeyed from Portugal. Her passing was a rude and sad surprise to the few of her set, as she had so long withstood the annual rainy season infections.

The couple had no children.

Having command over such a large territory and its outcomes, Señor Eduardo needed the peace of mind and ministrations of a comely woman. So two miserable years after his beloved wife was buried, he took in a native Taino named Casiguaya as housekeeper and, inevitably, lover.

Casiguaya had lost her husband to white-man-poison. Then, as Taino say, she lost her womb in birthing her baby girl Ramiya for the dead drunkard. Though sullen of mien, three years later she was still beautiful enough that El Señor fell for her and took she and child, Ramiya, into his home.

Treated the girl like a daughter and some say he same way loved her. And although it's unsafe to trust every word, this could be true.

Ashaki

ASHAKI, as her West African name suggests, was beautiful indeed. She was a fourteen-year-old, Haitian-born African who trekked to Santo Domingo with her parents during cane cutting seasons. There, in this or that plantation, they lived like chattel slaves for half of enough wages—though better than in Haiti where slavery was still okay.

Black beauty apart, Ashaki was a fearless girl. Old enough to know better, she squared eyes with any and everyone and spoke her mind. As for her remarks, backed up by a skeptical look, a favorite was "You don't frighten me!" Still, more than all else—main challenge to her parents and the world of men—Ashaki was supremely nubile.

Just after dusk of their second day of slaving, her parents each received from their foreman a package with a written sheet-paper. "Dis here from de hacienda," said the burly fellow-Haitian, "if you ent amount f'r read de paper, I learn it f'r tell you. Den mark in yuh X de okay." With the recent influx of stronger, Jamaican cutters, the man was working on his English.

Ashaki's parents didn't need to read and decipher. They could see and count well enough. So after realizing they each had twice the money they might have earned in their intended three months of cane-cutting, they did not hesitate to make their mark. They so grasped the situation, next afternoon, while every other cutter was toiling and tasking, they were treading the forest track back to their homey shack in Haiti, happily bearing one less burden.

Andaluza Ashaki Pinheiro

ANDALUZA ASHAKI PINHEIRO then, was the consequence of El Señor inviting Ashaki to work in the hacienda's kitchen. El Señor, at his age and with his lifestyle, had grown needful for reassurance about his manly vigor.

Andaluza grew up in the hacienda playing with Ramiya. Four or so years apart, little girls together, sometimes one's boss, sometimes the other's keeper, Ramiya and Andaluza were constant companions.

A few years later Ramiya's mother died from a deep-down *tabança* at missing her drunkard lover. For El Señor, a man of fifty plus years of good, even self-indulgent living, this was a profoundly depressing turn. That he had now lost a second 'wife' decided him to leave the cursed island for more promising, or at least healthier, pastures. As it turned out, correspondence with friends in high places suggested rowdy, cosmopolitan Trinidad as the best opportunity for him to continue being rich, privileged, and in charge—his God-given way of life.

Like the Spanish melody for which she was named, Andaluza was growing up so beautiful, smart, and charming, that when he decided to abandon that Isle of Unhappy Memories, although it was unthinkable that he take along her still young, beautiful, and pleasurable African mother, Ashaki, El Señor couldn't bear to leave behind his own exceptional half-Portuguese, mud-colored daughter.

Same as he couldn't desert his departed lover's pure Taino girl.

So El Señor Eduardo didn't.

He sold his sugar plantation and all goods and chattel within that he controlled. Made an exceedingly happy profit, and with his varicolored family emigrated to the Land of the Hummingbirds, where he settled down in the southern foothills of the Northern range in what was then countryside. There, Mr. Eduardo Gaspar Pinheiro built them a stylish ten-room bungalow with its own petrol-powered electricity generator—in those days, a flamboyant appliance indeed.

Itself furnished with every modern convenience, the bungalow had a large living room with adjoining dining room; a private study appointed with mahogany panels; an independent, fully-equipped master bedroom, and three others that shared two toilets and showers; a master kitchen with an adequate pantry and storeroom; and a separate servant's chamber. All of which went with Mr. Pinheiro's wealth and social stature. Then to make his home a cultural destination for the upper brackets, he created and sponsored a Society for Indigenous Peoples and appointed himself director authorized to disburse five thousand dollars to selected Needful.

Within weeks, among the echelons that mattered, he was instantly famous for his outstanding social and multicultural parties. As the wife of the Energy Minister declared during the first SIP presentation ceremony: "I have to point out to all a' all-you that Mr. Pinheiro's generosity to this important cause is example for all a' we. So we owe him every courtesy and support as we help popularize the important contributions from, and of, we own indigenous folks. I talking about them aristocratic tribes like the Taino who so different to the more humble farming Arawaks. Then we have them isolationist Caribs who some say just naturally savage. Neither shall we forget, or ignore, the island-hopping Kalipuna traders in their dugouts. And we must make mention, too, of the cassava farine makers from Aripo who—"

Mrs. Gomes might have expanded on Native people even further, except that a tipsy nit-picker interrupted at this point. "Excuse me, Missis Minister," said she, "I just wanted to add, to say, that runaway African slaves in Arouca also made farine from cassava, and since they run away from oppression and live within the, I mean, survive by the same Native ways and means, I just saying that maybe, at least, I think they should count as indigenous too. Eh?"

Very attractive in a figure-hugging shocking-pink dress, a string of pale fat pearls lustrous against her dark skin, she was just making it clear to all and sundry that marriage to a white and well-connected Scottish banker was not, in any way, abandonment of her race.

Since arriving into the naughty tumble of Trinidadian high society in the fifties, and as it seemed to add a touch of the risqué to his persona, Eduardo had bestowed the moniker 'Darling Daughters' upon Ramiya and Andaluza. Yet the darlings shunned their father's circles with a vengeance. Ramiya's name for them was El Señor's Groupies. Andaluza's choice was The Titterers. This ambiguous attitude about Eduardo became one of the many matters the girls shared while caring for each other all through their teens and early twenties.

Andaluza attended expensive private primary and secondary schools and academically, if not socially, did well. Ramiya learned to read, do basic math, and loved the cooking classes. Still, she gave up on schooling at fifteen. Just stopped. Didn't put on the uniform one Monday morning. When asked why, she explained to a mildly amused Eduardo, "Well, I tired wasting time lock up in a cage, looking at people who talking too fast telling me 'bout thing I don't want to know. I prefer to stay home and practice mih cooking. And that's what I intend to do."

"Makes sense to me," agreed Eduardo, "European education is quite a sophisticated system. So many aspects to consider. Can't be expected to make sense to a primitive culture."

Another example of fast talk flying past her comprehension, Ramiya only understood, with great relief, that El Señor was not going to make a fuss about the matter.

Andaluza was nineteen, Ramiya four, five years older when Eduardo Gaspar Pinheiro finally tippled over from a life maybe too fully lived. For the first month or so after their father's burial—which was managed by who knows who—the girls, shocked into independence, leaned even more heavily on each other. Various men and women from Eduardo's clique ran the house and maybe his business. The girls didn't know exactly—to these people the front door had no lock, they came and went at will.

Then on a Saturday middle of the second month, the girls were in the kitchen cooking when a grey-haired, deeply-tanned white man wearing a blue-striped seersucker business suit rapped knuckles on the open door; he seemed another from the in-crowd. Protective as usual, Ramiya stepped in front Andaluza and said, "Yes?"

The man cleared his throat and said, "Can I come in?" His accent was uppity Trinidadian, his good grammar effortless as he spoke the whole of every little word.

Andaluza stepped out to Ramiya's side and said, "Who's you?"

"Oh yes," the man said, "I am in error here. I am Mr.

Eduardo Gaspar Pinheiro's lawyer. The deceased lawyer, that is to say. My name is Mr. Winston Coryat. Here is my card." He took from a pocket and offered.

Andaluza accepted the card, glanced at it, said, "Okay, come in. Have a seat there at the table."

Mr. Coryat pulled out a chair and sat at the kitchen table. He cleared his throat, clapped his hands together, and addressed Andaluza, "I take it you are Miss Pinheiro, am I right?"

"We is both Miss Pinheiro. We is both Mr. Pinheiro daughters," said Andaluza flatly.

"Ah! I see," said Mr. Coryat, holding her eyes while his fingers pulled a long brown envelope from an inside jacket pocket. "What I have here is the deceased last will and testament, which in essence, states that all of the deceased properties and values shall be bequeathed to his daughter, one Andaluza Ashaki Pinheiro. Ah! Yes, that is what it says, in essence." He cleared his throat and placed the envelope on the table.

Hands covering and squeezing her open mouth, Andaluza looked consternation to Ramiya. "You hear that?" she said to her. "You hear what he saying?"

Ramiya chuckled ironic. "You know how mih ears clean, girl," she said, moving in to hug her sister. "But you shouldn't be surprised. I ent."

Andaluza shrugged herself out of the embrace, looked Ramiya straight in her face, "But he leave everything to me. Nothing for you. That can't be right, Ramiya. That can't be."

Ramiya sucked her teeth dismissively, "Girl, what you

talking? El Señor always was for him blood ties. And truth be said, I don't mind not having he kinda blood in me. I never forget mih pagan blood name is Casiguaya, and that when Mami get sick, yuh father just send she back to she people in the bush. To this day I don't know she grave site. So why you don't go do yuh father business with he lawyer? I go be in mih room." Then, without a glance or word to Mr. Coryat, she stalked out of the kitchen. Left them to handling details of Andaluza's considerable inheritance.

Shanika Grant-Ali

SHANIKA GRANT-ALI'S father was Osman Ali, a coffee-colored Indian Muslim. Respected imam in his community, he was a trusted arbiter of disagreements and general propriety. Shanika's mother, Elizabeth Evelyn Grant is Creole Trini, cinnamon-brown with soft hair and an unflappable disposition. Working as teachers in the same primary school down South, they fell in love, got married and started a family. This was the mix-it-up eighties, 'Woman on the Base' the calypso about "*an Indian girl who tie up she belly and played a sweet, sweet melody*" had been a Carnival road-march.

Shanika was their first-born and two years later came the apple of his father's eyes, Ahmed, who, breaking three loving hearts, died of malaria at nine years old.

Other negative factors, though mainly extreme grief, led to Babu's disenchantment with his God—utterance of this blasphemy being said to his trusted wife, who uncharacteristically admonished, "Osman Ali! You better bite yuh tongue, man!"

Fleeing from Misfortune, the family emigrated to New York where they spent eleven industrious years missing home. The parents worked the usual West Indian system—two jobs, one for living expenses and one for saving towards a retirement home back in Trinidad and Tobago.

Shanika attended public high school, was inspired into art and showed prizewinning talent enough to be granted a partial scholarship to an Ivy League college. To which her parents wrote back, "Thank you very much. We appreciate the honor, but cannot afford our financial end of your generosity. Kindly pass this on to someone who can."

So instead, Shanika went to the State college offering the best art program. In three quick years, she graduated *cum laude* with a B.A. in Fine Arts at essentially no cost since she was a N.Y. state resident. She did have to pay subway fares to her after-school part-time caring for elderly ladies at a nursing home. That's where she got her first professional assignment: a portrait of frail but doughty, fun-loving, eighty-something twins.

Working from photographs, Shanika completed the eighteen by twenty-four-inch painting in two weeks. She imbued the piece with vibrancy. Splashes of red and gold in the outdoor autumn background. Positioned the twins in a loose semi-circle of hugs, arms about each other's shoulders. Spots of pink in their not-so-lined-as-current faces. Pupils black and sparkling bright in crinkly smiling eyes that looked straight at you. Bold, fearless, ready for thrills.

Two years later when Shanika left the nursing home job

to return with the family to T&T, she had made maybe a hundred paintings, mostly color portraits created from yellowing, black and white photographs fragile with fading memories. For some she got ten dollars. For others, she got as much as a hundred. Whatever they gave, she accepted; even when off and on, it was only a long tremulous hug.

The Friday that was her last day, staff and patients gave her a send-off party. A hearty affair with buntings and ribbons and silly hats and chocolate cakes and cream puffs. Someone brought a calypso CD of old timers like Lord Kitchener and the Mighty Terror and Lord Melody. Shanika showed them how to chip and wiggle-wine calypso-style and a few braver old ladies tried for a fun minute or two. At the end presents and addresses were exchanged, followed by cards and heartfelt tears with promises to keep in touch and whatever.

As the years passed, sweet memories notwithstanding, Shanika never did.

Vivion K Pinheiro

VIVION K PINHEIRO is the illegitimate son of Andaluza Ashaki Pinheiro—who never spoke about his father. A light-skinned, happy-go-lucky fellow ever seeking personal satisfaction, Vivion chose to ramble self-discovered paths. 'Peppers and Romance' is an account of his intrigues . . .

ooOoo

Peppers and Romance

AT A MOMENTARY PARTING OF THE LADEN CLOUDS, just as Vivion stepped outside, brilliant moonlight illuminated the quiet night. He slid the front door to until the lock clicked shut, then turned for the grass and rubber-tiled path that led to the front gate. Then all at once he was smiling ironic at the cartoon panel a beaming full moon presented him—*his shadow on the wall as a humpbacked scoundrel creeping away from a crime.*

But hold up right there! This full moon was lime-lighting a false scenario.

True. His backpack *was* crammed to its over-stressed zippers, and granted, he *was* sneaking out of his marvelous palace. But rather than villain of the plot, this time he was, more or less, the selfless gallant who—by leaving this most comfortable nest and fleeing into uncertainty—was saving a damsel from distress while, at the same time, keeping a parent sane. All of this valiant action being done with the sole aim of delivering his closest persons from the evils of bitterness and strife.

Yes! To Vivion a 'Hero' label sounded just about right.

Consider that practicing selfless restraint, he did not mention his personal need for breathing space. Neither did he bring up a commanding urge to breakout from the physic cage called Comfort in which he felt entrapped. And then standing out like a flare, there was the situation regarding his over-exuberant pepper-farm venture: due in equal parts to last year's experimenting and this year's favorable weather, in a few short weeks he'll be rewarded with five acres of ripe, high-grade produce. Five acres of ripe hot peppers! Hundreds of pounds of produce! All that abundance.

And only couple weeks ago, Vivion realized he had no working idea of how to effectively trade them.

As far as getting them off the trees and transport ready, he could depend on Mr. Maharaj, his head gardener, to get pickers and packers. But although months ago, he had seen the signs of a bumper crop, in his elation he had not taken the thought a step farther. He had not made arrangements with either wholesalers or large-scale vendors to deal with his successes.

Now, no matter Vivion's best moves, the endgame seemed doomed. He had one last play to make, but however that might turn out, right now it was time for a break, a reliever. So though disappointed to the max, he was leaving the troublesome scene to an emergency expert. A veteran who was swift at assessment and solution—who had worked for him since forever used to be an anxious day.

Mother, once more, would have to take care of his mess.

When he got to the gate cut into the two-foot thick hibiscus fence, the smile lines bracketing his broad mouth were curved grim and downward. He tightened his lips as he gently latched the gate and turned left into the moonlit gravel lane through the woods towards the main road. He paused there for a moment, drew in a deep breath and squared up his shoulders resolute, then was fast away.

Above him, black clouds were low and building, erratic beams of moonlight shone through, and a rising wind was playing pitch and toss with overhead branches, making their shadows restless as swelling waves. Quick strides pushing the road behind, Vivion kept best as possible within the branches' swaying shadows. Branches that rustled with damp whispers forecasting rain. Vivion had figured for that, though. The junction a mere quarter mile on, even if it did rain, he'd still have had time either to get a bus or a taxi— some sort of regular transport—or else get lucky. He did feel that whatever came up, he'd have time to manage it. Although—and he grinned at the thought—he didn't mind rain at all! Night was bad enough, but a wet night would definitely keep Shanika from coming after him, not his Nikki.

Regardless of weather, he didn't expect she would though—he had taken steps to make it so. He had left his study door closed, and the overhead light on, and the computer playing light classics as he did when busy. Also, since moving in six months ago, she had shown herself to be a late sleeper. And lastly, in consideration for over-concern at his sudden absence, he had left a note under the computer keyboard that read:

"Nikki, sweetheart, not to worry. Just a thing I have to do. Be back in a few that might take maybe three weeks, hgs&ksss."

Truth be told, he did have strongest feelings for this fine woman!

Arrived at the junction without incident, Vivion stood sheltered in the deep shadow of a giant mango Rose tree. Long minutes passed with him tense, waiting for what he didn't know. All at once he was feeling vulnerable. While getting here, not wanting to seem furtive to any who might've chanced on noticing, he had worked his will at not looking back. Right now though, just standing still, lurking in shadows, did not at all bolster that earlier strong-willed poise. Driven by a sudden frantic urgency, he just had to know if he had been followed. So he turned around and as far as squinted eyes could focus, searched the moonlit track he had walked. Then he blinked and closed his dried out eyes, rested them a bit before he had them again straining and staring through the opaque moonlight.

He took good time to check and double check and give tenuous doubts space to materialize. And after all that thorough effort, Vivion sighed and nodded as, in general, he had to agree with himself that everything was everything, that all seemed safe.

The gravel-covered track he had trod made the foot a 'T' with the asphalt paved main road, a blacker than black divide that curved to the left around a low rise fifteen or so yards away. From his present position under the aged mango Rose tree he was able to see headlights from traffic in both directions on the main road. On the other hand, anyone coming up the lane would eventually discover him. But on yet another hand, there were no trees or convenient shadows alongside the main road. He fidgeted for a bit before murmuring "Better safe than sorry" and started up the main road around the low rising curve. Up because that was the direction of the busy town, the nightlife place where taxis would be available even at this late hour. He walked and kept looking back until he was well out of line sight of the junction, and then stood there in the open. Again feeling exposed, Vivion made quick assessment of his surroundings and shrugged. Worse come to worst, he could jump down and hide in the deep roadside drain.

Right now all to do was wait.

His thoughts returned to Nikki and how she'd take his absence. She'd most likely blame Mother, assume the worst. See her as inciter supreme. Or she might paint herself as the thorn that pierced a beautiful mother-son balloon. With her painter's tendency, she'd create a tragic palette of hopeless colors. And she'd be dead wrong.

Mother wasn't so.

At the beginning when they first got together, Vivion was showing her some photos of his sweetheart, and as he halfway expected, a main concern was his sweetheart's milk-in-the-coffee brown skin. "She kinda dark, not so?" said

Mother as she took the photo and angled and refocused it to suit her critical vantage.

On it right away, Vivion invented: "That deep color is due to the sheen of Dougla skin. The natural oils from the mix of Indian and who ever. Nikki lighter brownish in real life."

Mother had moved on, assessing another shot. "She hair look nice though," she said. "How it so long and black and curly, hmm, it remind me of mih own"—tossing her salt-and-pepper mane back as she added—"when I was younger."

By the end of that visit Vivion found out that Nikki's independent spirit also reminded Mother of her younger self. Which was seriously rare respect for a 'nowadays' woman, which was Mother's word substitute for decadent and worse. Another winner was that Nikki's special talent as a successful artist ruled out her using Vivion as a cash cow, a gullible catch that'd set her and her family on easy street. They were already there.

That sort of grasping woman had no chance with Mother; not with the hardships in sweat and soul she had survived to be who she was, and of which she spoke in aloe-bitter tones.

Vivion's biggest surprise was a gradual understanding that Mother's chief objection to his woman had more to do with her preference to them living together unmarried. To his mother's mind this clearly showed how Nikki had been influenced by slack, foreign ideas she picked up at those New York schools he told her of.

Fact is, it wasn't 'foreign ideas' at all. From what Nikki

had related to him, most likely it was the unexpected money resulting from her talent that was sort of the spoiler. On the one hand it firmed up her stubborn, independent nature to do things her way, or no way. On the other, it spurred her sympathetic spirit, making an instinctive generosity casual— she could always sell another painting if needs be.

Which was hardly likely.

Because Nikki's major cash flow bubbled from kind acts done years before while she part-timed in a nursing home for senior ladies in New York City. There, for fun much more than profit, she painted pleasing portraits of her charges. Developed a technique of invigorating the paintings—pieces that were always well-received, and much appreciated. Built herself a reputation and a following. Then as it happened, with sad goodbyes to all that, she returned home to Trinidad with her parents.

It turned out, though, that financed by one of those elderly ladies, a family member—a brother or a son— opened a business in Toronto making nostalgic portraits similar to Nikki's. "Memory Lane Portraits" was its name. Two years after being back home, in the packet of legal documents and a postage-paid return envelope they sent, lawyers explained that since she was the inspiration and model for the business, the original financier had insisted Nikki receive a ten percent share of all profits. The letter went on that the majority shareholder group was eager to have the documents signed, sealed, and delivered ASAP.

A postscript stated that the group regretted being unable to travel to her beautiful island nation and take care of the matter personally.

Nikki's father Osman, in imam mode, thought he smelled a rat in the urgent tone of business, but hadn't the energy to pursue his suspicions. So his thinking being that ten percent of anything is better than no percentage at all, he advised Nikki to sign and send the papers.

This backed by an "Okay" from a lawyer uncle, Nikki signed the papers. Two months later she got a check from Canadian Royal Bank. A cover note explained:

> The attached cheque is due part payment of profits from Memory Lane Portraits; Inc. for the last two years. Because of legal clauses regarding payout limitations, checks of similar amounts payable to you, or your legally designated payee, will be arriving on or about the second Monday of every third month. After three years, due payments will then equal the current market value of Memory Lane Portraits; Inc.
>
> Thanks for your business. Have a nice day!

The check was for twenty thousand Canadian dollars!

Nikki didn't bother multiplying by five point whatever for exchanged T&T dollars. Past pure astonishment, she was moved to shedding grateful tears as a humbling question overwhelmed her mind, "Who was that sweet and generous old lady?"

When a few weeks ago it first occurred to him that he was unprepared for the expected bounteous crop, Vivion took his concerns to Mother. Found her in the rocking chair on the verandah, cold of eye and standoffish. "You couldn't see that coming?" she said. "Well I could see it coming like a slap to mih face. But you have eyes for something else. Not so? You like a jackass led by a short carrot," she goaded. "You not seeing *this* far ahead!" She snapped fingers for emphasis.

Vivion breathed out his patience as a sigh. "Okay, Mother, you're right. No need to gloat. I didn't think ahead. I was so caught up in the day-to-day. I just didn't think—"

Mother interrupted, "So your girlfriend couldn't remind you? I hear she living there day-to-day, like a owner. What you having she there for? Eh? Is saltfish you like so?"

Vivion thought to stop right there. Not say another word. He now realized her heading. A couple months after Nikki moved in, Mother's displeasure had turned to puzzlement when Vivion bragged that in New York Nikki used to get thousands of dollars for her paintings, that her work was praised in important magazines, and that she had a following of cognoscenti up there.

With furrowed doubting brow, Mother had asked, "You serious, Vivion? Who dream you that dream? Anybody could make up fairy tale. You think everybody who go New York find a fortune? You think it have gold in the streets up there?"

Vivion had kept check of his temper. He didn't say that she herself had bragged about the opportunities found in New York. For who had the brains to see, she had proclaimed, a gold mine of ideas was there. It was where she got her idea to build the block of two-storied two-and-three bedroom townhouses that made her rich! It was there in New York that she got the contractors and building plans from Trinidadian immigrants turned US citizens!

And more important than all that, it was most likely in New York that she met the pale-skinned father he had never known!

But though angry and defensive, Vivion didn't say any of that. Instead, he insisted, "This is not old talk, Mother. Is bald truth. I checked on the Web. It there for anyone to see. People, experts, say she paints portraits that capture nostalgia. I could tell you the quotes by heart. One critic say, 'she returns youth and bright promise to aging faces.' Is about how she uses color and brush strokes and stuff like that. Technique and whatnot. I don't really know. But clients love what she does. They go crazy for it. They pass over the big bucks. Mother, look. You gotta get this. The two years since they moved up to Tamana Valley, Shanika Grant-Ali, yes, my Nikki at twenty-five is most likely the richest young woman in the county. I mean, who you think pay for that eight-room ranch house she family living in. Who you think pay Dr. Mason for the land to build on?"

Mother sucked frothy contempt through her teeth. "So why don't she take she rich backside and go live she rich life with she own rich kind. Why she have to move in with my gadabout son in the fancy future-house that I build for him?"

"Mother, don't bring up that stale house stuff. I know what I do same way I know what you do. And about Nikki, we went through that already. I tell you the truth that she moved in because I didn't mind, because I couldn't tell she not to, and because I weak for her. That's it! Simple!"

"So you happy she here then?"

"Yes, Mother, most of the time. Sometimes I still like mih solitude. But listen to me!" he pleaded as she had started for the back door screen. "You gotta listen and believe!" he said earnestly when she stopped and turned around. "We get along. We really do. She is the first woman I know who let me be me, myself. She totally on my side. She at ease around me. Public or private, she bold enough and makes moves I like. We give each other space when we busy into we own thing. When we have to. She like to work upstairs in the back room facing the creek and the forests. The tall immortelle trees swaying mournful. I prefer down here looking at the openness. That's what I like about her. Plus other things. Like how both a' we like to cook. She know every Indian dish on the planet. Some she learn from she father, some she invent. To me that's great. Listen to this. Sometimes we cooking different meals and exchanging with each other to taste and judge. It does be so funny. You should hear what does come up when we try to describe tastes and smells. The comparisons alone, you have to laugh. I telling you, Mother, we does have a good time. Really."

"So then why you don't marry up this woman and make she respectable? Why you don't give me a respectable grandchild and give she a respectable child instead of letting people throw bad eyes at she for living here in sin with a no account man."

At that, Vivion's ire fought back. No account! Sin! Who, what was she talking about? She who only believed in Eshu and Haitian obeah. She who has a mudada voodoo doll sitting over her mirror. Who was she to make judgment? In any case, what he cared about sin would prance through a needle's eye. And as far as no account went, not cent from her, he had earned himself a free University education. He also had had choice whether or not to represent the nation in international athletics. That don't sound so no account.

Still braking his exasperation, he stood up and said, "Mother let's not get into that, okay. You might have a thing about people and respect. Especially about bastards. But I don't. I grow up bastard and I doing fine—"

"—only because of yuh mother's efforts at the expense of she pride and dignity!" she interjected.

Temper taking over all at once, Vivion got loud saying, "Mother, I say we *not* going down that road. I know you went through harsh times. You suffered. You went to New York on vacation and come back with a light-skinned baby boy, a Yankee child that is me. I get that. You come back to social disdain and so forth. That was how it was in your day. But that time pass. It ent so no more. It not all the way gone but it on the way out. Look, I understand why Nikki parents abandon ship because she living with me. That's their choice made from their ancient ethics of their ancient times and religions. In a way they same as you. But since they don't feed or fend for she or me, I just don't give a damn! Why should I? Why should we?"

"So is you and she against the world, eh? And that's why you feeling big tall man enough to shout down yuh own mother?"

And that's how that discussion had died, or more exactly, passed out from exhaustion, to be revived and contested some other day.

Tuesday a week later Mother surprised him. It was a sticky afternoon and he was staring blankly at the dark green hibiscus fence that shielded the front of the ground floor from the road when, with her white wide-brimmed hat aslant at the usual rakish angle, she pushed open the fence gate and sashayed through. Vivion smiled. A dainty picture in a sleeveless red dress with a shirred full skirt, she looked half her age. Loosely knotted at her narrow waist, accenting her hour-glass figure, was a wide black belt. White socks and black sneakers completed the outfit. From walk to wear, he could see her good mood.

Knowing that although she had the password, she'd still ring the doorbell, he sprang up and went to the door so that as she got there he opened it and smiling wide, greeted, "Hey, Mamita. What *la Señora en rojo* doing looking so fine out here among the forests and farms? Come on in out of the heat."

Despite his awful, affected accent, she entered, unpinned her hat from her hair and fanned her face with it. She replied, "So I have to explain mih self for taking a stroll?" Her tone, though, was playful.

Vivion turned from the fridge and exclaimed, "Mother! Don't tell me you walk all the way from the junction."

"Well, what else to do? After I get off the bus, ten minutes I waiting for a taxi and none ent coming. In this heat to boot. So I start walking and that was that. I end up reaching."

Vivion handed her a tall glass of cool coconut water with a dash of Angostura bitters. "Poor thing," he said. "This will make the pretty little lady feel better."

"Thanks, boy," she said, "coconut water is a true thirst blessing," and downed half of her drink. Then she put the glass on the table and gathered up her hair in a bun. "Sometimes this hair could be a burden, you know," she declared with a sigh as she reclined on the cool leather couch.

As they sat and chatted and drank beverages, it occurred to Vivion that Mother had come by on the only day that Nikki was away socializing with her artsy folks. He got to wondering if it was deliberate, the thought so distracting him that he didn't hear a question put to him. "What you say, Mother?"

"Is not what I said. Is what have you other minded? What's on yuh mind?"

"Ent nothing, Mother," he said. Then, as he created an appropriate one, added, "Nothing bad. I was only wondering if you in a mood to see how the peppers thing working out. Would you? Please?"

"In this heat?" said Mother, her raised eyebrows almost joining in protest.

"It will only take five, ten minutes and look at the thermometer. It saying 80 F. So it cooling down some already," he returned with a clever cower that was part disappointed shrug and part accusation.

"Well, okay," surrendered his mother. "But not a minute more."

Vivion was overjoyed. This was her first visit since two years ago when earth-moving tractors had just finished forming beds and banks and drainage canals that converted open land into an organized garden. Now it was a well-functioning farm, a sea change difference from the fiascoes of the first year. The pepper project was all around wonderful, and success was in the air like a happiness buzz. In high spirits he was ready to show off the fruits of his ingenuity and determination.

As they were passing the bee hives, he crowed, "Mother! I telling you straight. Look at them hives. Best investment I could've made. Even I was only guessing it'd work. You have to admit you was thinking it wouldn't. Eh? Not so? Now look at how them pepper plants flowering. Eh! Lavish. Lavish is the only word. And you taste how the honey different, kinda—?"

"Vivion," Mother cut in with a voice dry as dust, "as far as I remember, it was me who buy those hives from a Chinese fella down by the wharf, and it was the same me who had Mr. Ramdeen workmen install them. That's all I remember 'bout *your* wonderful hives."

At which point atmosphere and ambience made it clear that the tour should end, so Vivion responded, "You feeling the heat like me? What you say we go back in the palace, eh? It definitely cooler in there."

Head held high, Mother cut him an ambiguous look, tossed loose strands of her salt-and-pepper mane from her shoulder, and started for the turf-grass track back to the house.

Both of them sweating beads, sneakers off on the back porch, they slid the blind open and entered the air-conditioned living space. Vivion went to the fridge, poured them tall glasses of their preferences; Mother drinking fresh coconut water with a dash of bitters, he the same with a heaped tablespoon of powered skim milk swizzled in.

Then they sat savoring the quiet cool as from outside came sounds of Nature going about business. The wind creaking branches that shrieked their glee like school children at recess. A woodpecker knocking out a nest somewhere in the bamboo stool by the creek. Pecking with a rhythm, four or five volleys of a neat quick rat-a-tat-a-tat, then a stop so sudden your ears missed the beat and waited. Hoping, as maybe the working bird took a look around, checking if he had drawn unwelcome attention.

Then he's back on the job. Rat-a-tat-a-tat-a-tat.

"I wish that bird would stop its confounded racket!"

The protest startled through Vivion's reverie, "What?"

"That blasted bird is hammering me a headache!" said Mother.

And Vivion realized that she was still vexed. Maybe about the bees. For the first time it occurred to him that this might be the reason she had shunned the palace. But he couldn't have this. Right away, he decided to make amends. Things were going too blue skies nice to have such a slight matter throw up clouds.

"Mother," he said. "I want to say I didn't forget how much you did with the bees and the house and everything. Is that I just don't talk about it. But I does *feel* about it. And one thing certain, I feel grateful."

He spoke the last like a plea and watched as she sipped her coconut water while over the rim of her glass she gave him a long complicated look; at the same time soft and indulgent, yet with a tinge of petulance.

Eyes holding his, she sipped and sipped her drink then,

finally, looked away as she said, "Look, boy. Don't take no horrors from me. Okay. Is only the heat that get to me. I know you appreciate what I do. Is just . . . " and she left the thought hanging there in the quiet room.

Even the woodpecker was waiting in silence.

At which Vivion, feeling forgiven, said cheekily, "I know what. Is the smell of them bee-hive honey that you set off. Them bees' product too sweet even for you."

Seeing her genuine smile, he went over to her, bussed her head and said, "What you say I give the old Queen a refill, eh?" and took the glass from her hand.

Smile grown wider, she said with mock severity, "You'd better stop that stupidness right there, right now. One thing I too old for is foolery!"

"But Mother you know I ent joking. You know you is the queen around here. You know any and everybody will do whatever for you. Goes without saying. Me! Moi! All I have is ideas. Like putting in we own bees to do we own pollinating. That is part of my Integrated Self-Supportive System for superior ecological management. You know, like using the river for irrigation and hydroelectric energy, like setting up the overflow as a tilapia fish pond. Remember when I tried that? But what ever I think up, I never forget you is mih M.M.I.H. My own personal Mistress of Making It Happen."

Merry as a songbird, he hugged his mother around her neck, and although she made no accommodation to ease the awkward embrace, Vivion could breathe in her pleasure.

Outside, the woodpecker returned to nest building.

ooOoo

THE WHINE OF AN ENGINE coming up behind him bored through his reverie, so Vivion resettled his backpack and began slowly walking away from the approaching vehicle in the dark. Too fast to make out anything, sudden headlights briefly swept over the trees lining the road as a sports car screeched around the bend changing gears as it roared on uptown. Vivion watched the diminishing red lights thoughtfully and walked a few paces further away from the bend and swung his backpack to the ground. Figured he'd rest there for a bit. No sense in walking when one might get a ride.

The wind had died, the night calm about it, the air cool and pregnant heavy. Getting ready to release. All the noisy dark-time creatures—the birds, the bugs, the frogs—were being quiet in cozy protected places. Vivion thought about taking out the thin plastic poncho in his backpack. He counted off 'should I, should I not' on his fingers twice, and was about to go for a two-out-of-three decision when there came faint sounds of an engine. Steadily approaching, it was heading his way. Vivion hoisted the backpack and again began walking away from the vehicle. A few steps on, the headlights swung over him, gilding the black roadway further on as Vivion stepped into its grassy edge, giving way. The vehicle seemed to slow as it passed. Then it geared down and stopped altogether. The driver side door opened, a figure poked its head out and looked back. A voice, loud in the still night, asked, "That you, Reds?"

Startled, Vivion said, "Who dat?"

Enough to reassure the driver, who said, "Come on, Reds. You can't hide. Long and lingay like you is, you is the onliest fella could wear a backpack and still swagger."

Vivion went up to the vehicle, a covered jeep, saw the Trinidad and Tobago coat of arms printed above an Armed Forces insignia. He looked in through the window at a grinning face he recognized. "Carlos Riviera!" he exclaimed. "Where in Hell you heading this time a' night?"

"Is I should be asking that," said Carlos, laughing hearty. "Come on in, man. Come in. Where _you_ going?"

"Piarco," said Vivion as he slammed the door shut.

"What! You flying out?"

"With Com Ex, if I get there before one o'clock."

"Com Ex, eh," said Carlos with a sly glance that might have winked. "No problemo, mih Bro. Is only just going on midnight. We have lotsa time, and for any package named Reds Pinheiro, Piarco is directly on my way. Leh we go."

And grinning like tricksters, off they went.

Carlos Riviera was a classmate of his in elementary

school when he was ten or eleven. Gifted with a wicked insightful wit, Carlos attacked and bullied with scathing on-the-mark comments that stung to the bone and always provoked derisive laughter. Be it education, family matters, or personal hygiene, you pitied the fool who messed with Carlos. Pitied him while laughing your ass off. For Carlos could be funny, sharp, but most of all he was nasty.

Vivion never tangled with him. He knew better. Took no chances. As one of two boys in the class who could never present a father, he was too vulnerable. So he made nice with Carlos; bought him sweetmeats from the schoolyard vendors—especially the spicy Indian delicacies he liked; showed him done homework to copy when asked; and sensibly, stayed clear of him when he was being vicious.

Vivion lost touch with him when, as with most of the other boys, at twelve Carlos went on to high school. Vivion, arranged by Mother, got a show job as a technical assistant in an agricultural experimental station—a connection that allowed him to pursue academic interests in his own whimsical way. Several years later they met again in Piarco airport when Vivion was returning from Caracas. Carlos, grown up broad-shouldered, mustached, and cocky as ever, worked there as a Customs agent. After one swift glance that signaled 'collusion' they did not acknowledge each other. That same weekend though, they hung out sipping quality brandy at a birthday party because Carlos had allowed his buddy to pass through without paying duty on several expensive items: perfume for his mother and self; a battery-powered transistor pocket radio and a pair of proper-sized sneakers also for self; and four bottles of pricey brandy unavailable in T&T. That sealed a casual friendship that remained just so and they were always hearty with each other upon meeting.

And now this night! Talk about luck!

Vivion got into updating first, asking "So how come you in the Army?"

"Is a long story, man," Carlos began, "and it just showing how life could twist from easy to hard. How long it is I ent see you? Four, five years? Well boy, Christmas three years now I get married to this woman, but by six quick months all the happiness finish and done. Long story short, she wanted to be a stay-at-home wife and for me to get a regular nine-to-five with a future. She didn't see me playing football for a living. Is not that I wasn't good, yu'know. I mean for one thing, I get pick on the National side and was getting a nice, nice stipend. Mid-field, right or left side, the man distributing the ball. That was me. A standout in every game. Pictures in the papers every game. You know how it is. I was good, in mih prime, and comfortable. And that probably was the trouble. I was so comfortable, when time to change and adjust to married life, I just couldn't accustom mih-self to any inside desk job. Was like I in a cage, if you know what I mean? Couldn't keep one more than a month or two. So a year after we exchange rings and all that, she leave me for a politician fella, a snake-in-the-grass who used to visit while I playing football in the savannah. But me ent no fighter. Yuh can't sweeten love once it sour. She ask for divorce, I give she divorce. Officially was a no fault thing. But to make it convincing and quick I take all the blame. I tell the judge I was away from home too much and that kinda thing. But maybe that divorce make a bend in mih luck, 'cause like a charm, right after that happen, I get papers from the Army. I had put in the application many months before and did already forget it. But that's how it work out, and the army is where I been ever since. Is two years and counting since I feeling more and more comfortable. In fact thing so good I have a pickney on the way, six months in the belly. This is a half-Spanish sweetie-pie from Princess Town . . . "

Listening with one ear, Vivion hid his surprise at the story. Not so much the detail of love gone astray, but the bitterness with which Carlos spoke of his ex-wife. The way he never mentioned her name, and said 'she' like it tasted nasty on his tongue. The tale's overall peevish tabança. In truth, Carlos had become a different person. He got old too quick. It was as if he had used up all his humor during his youth, wasted it.

In elementary school, that most challenging place, he was a jep Tattoo—small, black, and lethal. He had earned the respect of bigger, older classmates; each one of them a bully in his own special style. Now Carlos had assumed surrendered ways, with hesitant voice and cynical patience. Gone was his ebullience, his torrent of snickers as he built up the scene before he dropped a bombshell jibe or insult. Now he sounded like a penitent under the weight of the world's woes, a make-do man accepting the countless sins committed against him.

" . . . is how it stand right now. Well man, that's mih life to date. But is like I doing all the talking, eh. So tell me about yourself. What's going on with you? This time Sunday night, where you off to?"

"No drama there, man," said Vivion, "I have some business in Barbados and I getting a freebee from mih friend who flying the Com Ex cargo plane." His tone and the leer he slid to Carlos, though, suggested a sultry female bracket all around 'business' as he continued talking. No mentioning that he was flying on to New York to try and solve a major problem. No mention at all of his pepper plantation frustrations. Instead, he brought up topics of slight significance—gossip, politics, popular calypsoes about the latest scandals. He made chat for light listening as he noted their progress along the dark, empty roadway. He stuck to school days' anecdotes, choosing and shaping his telling so that the final episode would conclude, more or less, at the entrance of the steadily nearing airport.

ooOoo

THE DRIZZLE THAT HAD PROMISED much more started as Vivion entered the quiet, vaulted space of the public waiting hall and paused just inside the door. Along the far wall, of the dozen or so business cages, only one was lit though he could see no one at window. He strolled on into the hall, veering left past a sizeable cubicle formed from two money exchange booths. Their signs stated business hours were 8 a.m. to 12 p.m. daily. He continued towards the far wall and there was his ride to New York—Charles Thomas Tyson, Tommy Tyson to his closest—sitting on a bench under a sign that said, 'No Entry - Pilots Lounge'. Just as he said he'd be.

He was absorbed reading a magazine.

Vivion approached him from behind, tapped him on the shoulder and greeted, "Tommy Tyson! So mih brother still trying to improve the I.Q, eh!"

"And you still minding people business?" said a smiling Tommy as he stood up all of his always surprising length, then stooped to clasp hands that were pulled into a one-shouldered hug.

He smelled warm and pleasant, like fresh made bread.

"You know me. Always wanted to be a private eye."

"You trying to say *maccoe*! Not so?" said Tommy as he lead them through the door over which was the label 'No Entry - Pilots Lounge'. "Anyhow, let's get going. Is never too early when it come to Immigration."

Vivion and Tommy met in first year Chemistry at U.W.I and became buddies—Tommy since then being the one person he regarded as 'Friend'. At the outset, they were only notable in being the most successful athletes in the class; Vivion a lanky six-foot-four champion quarter-miler, Tommy a lithe and muscular six-foot-seven who was the premium basketball forward on the University's top squad. It soon turned out that they had even more in common: like quick minds and a tendency to reticence; Tommy's claim to be born bashful; Vivion, self-taught since early, admitting to awkwardness in a peopled class room. There were other shared interests, like Science Fiction, and Zen Buddhism, and Sherlock Holmes and popular music, local and foreign. Yet, they gravitated towards each other at first mainly because they were both excellent at Chemistry, jockeying with each other for first place in monthly tests. By the second term, after sharing textbooks and stories and ideas in general, they had grown close. Enough for Vivion to learn that behind Tommy's shyness was a soft-spoken prankster with a penchant for making his conscience's dictates happen—a student who, by snail mail, sent to every one of

his classmates his well-researched Xerox printouts of the
most likely questions for a coming final test, and did so
because he thought the professor was an incompetent.
Another side of Tommy was his sponge-like memory that
he used to absorb the season's calypsoes and render them
during study breaks if begged by the female students.
Among jealous fellows who dismissed his manner as a
wussy gimmick, the feeling persisted that with Tommy,
sometimes the persuasion was infinitely more intimate.

Then leaving University in '06 with honors in Chemistry
and Zoology, Tommy surprised the class by going to flying
school in Florida; seems that his dream was always to fly the
endless skies. He earned his license in a couple years, during
which time he met and became co-pilot with an American
classmate to whom he promised togetherness through
sickness, health, and much, much more. A happy couple,
they now had a true pair of youngsters—a boy and a girl—
and maintained nice homes in Siparia, South Trinidad and
New Jersey, USA.

Tommy told Vivion to make himself comfortable and
went up front with his flight crew. A few minutes later they
were off, the plane climbing while it curved noticeably
before settling down to a steady drone towards its
destination.

With an intention to grab some shuteye, Vivion took
Tommy's advice to the letter. He pulled up the armrests of a
middle row of four seats, and with the help of several
pillows from an upright cabin, provided himself all the
comfort available.

Sometime later, awakening with a dry mouth and a need to pee, he rolled off his makeshift bed and started for the bathroom back of the plane, only to realize what had roused him. Passing through a patch of rough weather, the groaning aircraft was bouncing and shuddering as it slapped over turbulent airwaves. Vivion stumbled onwards into the bathroom, made a mess around the bowl, zipped up himself and managed back to his seat. Then all desire to sleep gone, he fastened his seat belt and readied his soul to endure.

He found himself comparing this current bumpy ride to his first run with Tommy six years ago. He had been running from an entanglement that was all the way wrong since an early abortion was such the more appropriate option. A backwoods half-Spanish first-year UWI student, she was a passing fancy who too soon gave Vivion the shudders. Then when they were talking about it, sly-eyeing him from under thick black false eyelashes, she said, "Well, Vivion, Mamita say is better I keep it 'causc I have to start thinking about mih-self a li'l bit more. And you know how I love you so much, too. Right?"

Which, to Vivion, made further discussion wasted breath.

So he went to a doctor he knew from campus—Sammy Camacho, an easy going, paunchy, Indian-looking sallow-skinned man, a seventies Mona graduate. His father was one of the Portuguese Camachos and made his money from wholesale merchandising. Sammy's mother was a still-striving though wealthy Hindu who owned and operated 'Spices, Curries, & Condiments', a one-door store half a block from the City market.

So by color and cash-clout Sammy was born to and fitted well into the country's upper crust. Vivion had his ear and favor mostly because of Mother's wealth and ancestry. Although she attended their annual cultural events, Mother never spoke well of them afterwards. Was catty about their clothes and looks and health and even their children's prospects. The basic truth was her bitterness at how these fine folks chose to ignore her mother's African blood and celebrated only her father's Portuguese roots. They never included her middle name, Ashaki, on their invitations.

Vivion had endured sort of similar distress at University when it came to explaining himself color-wise and fatherless.

So regarding 'Miss Sly Eyes' he explained the situation and paid friend Sammy, the doctor, for the procedure. He tried to add something extra to have the secretary call the good student and command in no nonsense medical vernacular that the doctor expected her in on so-and-so date, at so-and-so time.

Sammy would have nothing of the sort. "No! No! Vivion," he said. "Intimidation not necessary at all. I making the call mih self and I using another persuasion. As a government physician privy to medical records of anyone with an STD, I sorry to say, Miss, but I just find out you might be infect—"

"You making joke!" Vivion cut in, "You intend to tell she I have VD?"

"No. No. I telling she that her name has been mentioned as a recent sexual contact and she should come in and discuss her options."

"Whew! That sound better, much better," said Vivion.

"Come on, man," said Sammy, "you expect me to sully yuh family name?" he chuckled and continued, "In fact, you want to know a simple psych that'll have any young woman, any woman at all, running to the doctor to rid she-self of a fetus?"

Vivion allowed, "Once is not a hollow voice saying, 'Abort Me Sesame'!"

Sammy showed him a professional, deprecating surgeon's smile. "Listen," he began, "in med. school the fellas used to call it the Klinefelter procedure. Is like this. Klinefelter's is a genetic condition. The baby born with XXY or XYY instead of the normal XX or XY. See? That mean it born to be either over-manly or over-womanly. And this can show up as a man with breasts or a female with extra organs, if you know where I mean. So if thing happen and you want to get rid of it, all you have to tell the unwilling woman is that you have Klinefelter syndrome. And then you explain what it is! You get me?"

"I could well see that frightening off a woman," said Vivion, "that's unless she desperate enough not to mind a few problems," he ended in a doubtful tone.

"Man, don't even think that," chided Sammy, "who woman nowadays looking for them kinda problems? She thinking moo-moo once she hear the word genetic. People ignorant like cow, boy. Anyhow, professional courtesy and all that. As family, you only paying for materials and equipment. End of story."

Which was kinda convincing, too. So Vivion shook

hands and left the matter to Sammy's adequate purview.

That same evening he also made arrangements with Tommy for a ride two days before the operation's due date, and after explaining that he'd be staying by a mate in Brooklyn, agreed to New Jersey as destination after Tommy explained the conveniences of Liberty air—

"How you managing the bronco busting?" came Tommy's voice from overhead and behind, startling him.

"You just gimme the biggest jolt yet, man," Vivion laughed.

"You showing good reflexes. I just checking," said Tommy, grinning as he came around and sat beside Vivion. "So what you think about them Indians? Tendulkar in particular?"

"Who? What you talking about?"

"Cricket, man. You don't follow cricket?" sounding it outrageous as if Vivion had forsaken sunshine and fresh air.

"Nah, man."

"But Reds, you used to play in UWI. You was a fine cricketer. Middle batting order, good fielder with speed and sweet reflexes. Best all rounder two years straight. That was you, Reds. So man, what happen?"

"I was just going through a phase those days, I suppose. Plus cricket was easier than training for quarter miles. Easier than any kind of championship running, in truth. Once I got to mid-forty times, they start expecting me to be a professional. Like a racehorse. Tommy, my man, this might surprise you, but horse is no part of my gene pool. And anyhow, you know how me and hard work never did sit on the same bench. I mean, that coach Flint was serious. The 'D' in he DNA must stand for Diligence. Or Doggedness. Most likely 'hard-ass' as a concept was created 'cause of him."

His shoulders in spasms of up-and-down jerking said that Tommy was laughing, and as always, his odd noiseless way of expressing mirth sweetened the humor for Vivion like a squeeze of lime juice in raw honey, and right away had him chuckling too.

They chatted about this and that until, somehow, the conversation meandered around to Tommy asking, "So why you don't settle down with some fine woman and create some replicas? Is one of the best jobs on earth. It can't be cost and you wouldn't have to work. Not with a moms like yours who owning apartment complex in the pricey part of town and dotes on her only son. And why shouldn't she? Look at yuh self. Over the halfway mark on straight line to thirty. Colored a shade of ruddy brown calmed by a splash of cream. Unusual, but nice. Athletic build on a solid frame six foot and some. Nice face with high cheek bones under an intelligent head of curly, red hair. Personality cynical but not overbearing. Generous with an amused manner that'd make—"

"Keep that sweet song going, Tommy-boy," Vivion interjected, "I liking the pictures."

Tommy had never stopped, "—a blind dog happy. So, I asking, with all these attractive attributes, why you can't find some woman to make you whole?"

Vivion sent a furtive sideways glance at his friend and

saw that behind his lightness there was serious puzzlement, an earnestness that moved him to answer true. "Listen, man. I trying, okay! As we speak right now, I trying. If I could find a woman who can take me as me. As the real true me without pretence. I will take her to live with as long as she could stand it. I mean to say, I is not a stable fella. I get moods that take me over. Fight as hard as I can, they still bowl me down and I have to surrender, do as they want. Mother say somebody light a candle on mih head. Is a light blazing road for a restless jumbie. Is a real strong spirit that won't stay put or tied down. It does just take me over and I have to follow, break away to openness, point mih nose to sea breeze on high cliffs that look to the horizon. Is hard to put an innocent woman through that. To do it deliberately is plain wickedness."

"Vivion, boy. I hearing you, you know. But what about regular social needs and, and obligations, and so on? You still part of the community. You is a citizen. You have to give back what you get from it. Contribute. Is what you went to school for."

"Well, I don't know about all that," said Vivion, taking umbrage. "I think I carry mih-self through on mih own weight. All that conventional high-schooling I miss was the best thing ever happen. Don't forget I beat out everybody to win that free schol. Remember, I only take that test to UWI because I wanted to know more about Science and Philosophy and High Arts and stuff. Knowledge to live better is all I wanted. What I was always looking for was a system, a gimmick to gain personal freedom. Of every sort and form. Freedom to do as I wish, when I wish, once I not harming anyone else. That system was all I ever wanted. It was never elite schooling. I not into being schooled."

"I know what you mean, man," said Tommy, nodding solemn as a mortician.

Surprised, Vivion said, "You do?"

"Sure, Reds. Is a common dream, my brother. Is every youth-man dream. Tweak it here and there, but we all have this same identical impossible dream. Freedom without the discipline of commitment. Look man, you is my real true friend. I know you not page by page, but at least by chapters. You just like me. You keep it close. But more than most, I've scanned yuh play book. Look here, brother, three, four years ago, who supported you when you decide to build yuh see-through sombrero house—"

Vivion sucked his teeth and cut in: "Tommy! Is not a sombrero house. Is a self-sufficient—"

Tommy waved a dismissive hand as he continued, "Reds man, hear me out. Who bring down all that specialized equipment? The hydroelectric power machine. The miniature wind turbines. Yes, face it. Who with you when you get the fish farm idea, eh? Who dat dere? Yes, sir, was me, Tallboy Tommy Tyson. And then the peppers project come up. As usual, who behind you step for step? Deal with the facts, Reds. Straight and simple, you is a butterfly kinda fella. In a way, you is a cliché. Out there flitting about busy doing the pretty flowers. But you only playing. You not serious at all. You don't follow through with anything. Is always one new project or the other. You just playing the fields. You not into any real pollinating. No product. Nothing permanent. Why you think I put mih foot down when mih sister start bearing that heart-load for you?"

The tone in his best friend's manner had become upbraiding. Distressing the moment. All at once he was giving off a strong, musky, angry scent. So grabbing the opening to moderate the scene, Vivion said, "Which one?

Tommy, brow in puzzled frown began, "Wha—?" before a smile blossomed as he caught the play and finished, "the one that would've kicked the tail piece out yuh backbone!"

"—and you thought I was referring to your beautiful sisters, eh. What a sterling, protective brother! But now, all joke aside, which one?"

Still amused, Tommy shook his head, got up and said, "See you later, man. You being yuh self is all right with me. Sometimes, but only sometimes, I wish I had that, that aplomb. Is partly why I admire you. But to business now, they give you trouble at Immigration, just show them the Com Ex packet and yuh courier ID. That, with yuh Yankee passport, should relax them. But I don't expect trouble. So I'll see you in three weeks, Sunday night again. Right here. Eleven o'clock. Okay! Now take care."

"You too, man," said Vivion as they squeezed warm palms. Then Tommy, shoulders stooping, head bowed low to avoid the plane's ceiling, returned to his pilot's cabin.

Vivion knew an enormous surge of relief as Tommy went. He wiped sweaty palms on his trousers, although the guilt remained warm as he looked back the way Tommy had gone. For he well knew who was the sister in question. Hester, the middle one, it was she who'd shared nectar with him during her final term in high school—the affair stopping by mutual agreement after two narrow escapes quashed the sexual thrill they enjoyed from the illicit liaison.

Vivion shook his head slowly, musing, "Yes, boy, wild honey could sting, yu'know!"

ooOoo

NIKKI WOKE UP, PUSHED from her face the mass of unruly hair that was close to stifling. She was in midst of a mighty stretch when a slight discomfort in her lower belly seized attention, a muscle pull being her first anxious thought. But right away this was squashed by a sour burp that seemed to be lurking back of her throat, a suggestion that perhaps her friend might soon be here!

She sighed timid relief. For although very aware of the consequences, she had stopped taking her pill two months ago, and there remained a tiny nag in her head that worried about how Vivion would react to a pregnancy.

Her dominant identity—the determined, selfish, feisty majority of her—pushed back and shrugged off that concern. What ever happened was her decision, it argued. She was almost twenty-six years old with above-average looks and a talent that'd earn her more money than she'd ever need. All that considered, to make her contentment perfect she now wanted a baby, and maybe a family, and she had chosen him to be the father. Wasn't only that she truly liked him, but that he was such an exceptional match. In order of importance, he was intelligent, good-looking, educated, and a clear four inches taller than her five-eleven-and-a-half. Barefoot. Much lighter skinned than she, with nice hair and an offbeat sense of humor, he was also financially independent via his mother's real estate fortune. In final tally, any quartet of Muslim parents would've agreed that he was just the perfect mate for her. So with parental consensus or no, she'd be a fool not to recognize that.

As she showered, Vivion remained pleasant on her mind. She marveled, as usual, at his ingenuity in installing hot and cold, hard and soft water faucets in every of the four bathrooms and kitchen in the odd shaped, two-storied house, his 'palace' as he called it. She was still getting accustomed to the name but was impressed enough to see its appropriateness.

His rooftop was equipped with a thousand-gallon tank with extendible funnels for collecting rainwater. He had installed eight solar power panels to collect the sun's energy, and front and back of the house, two two-foot-vane windmills to harness wind power via turbines. Just the thought of his enterprise thrilled. It was the turn-on that moved her affection from romantic to deep admiration to wanting his child. Fruit don't fall far from the tree. Goat don't make sheep. With she and he as parents, the child had to be beautiful, well-formed, and bright. No doubt about it. Vivion Pinheiro was her true-to-life one-in-a-million and Nikki was resolved to keep it that way.

Around ten o'clock, she went down the inclined four-

foot wide rubberized perimeter around the walls—the only
stairs in the house were those from the engine-room/attic
space to the rooftop. Into the living-room kitchen area on
the ground floor she went directly, as usual, to the fridge
and poured herself a glass of fresh cow's milk, drank it
down. She burped coyly and nodded to her self-indulgence.
Snaking her neck, she murmured to no one, "Yes, darling,
pretty Nikki do *loves* she cold fresh cow milk!" and liked her
performance so much, she giggled.

When she entered his study Nikki found the computer's
green energy-saver light blinking and his bed unslept. Still
adjusting to his erratic habits, she figured he had bedded
down in a spare bedroom. Then checking both floors and
not finding him, she returned to the study and searching
more carefully, saw the note angled out from under the
computer. She read it and right away was pissed. She figured
it was the same old, expected story. Mother trying to run
Son's life and ruining it instead. Well that stale tale was due
for a modern twist. Her ire fired, strong woman in love,
Nikki then and there decided to confront the situation and
get it over with. She'd visit Missus Mother Pinheiro and
throw her cards on the table. She'd try to convince the old
lady that although not looking for a fight, she wasn't about
to let Vivion be persuaded, or driven, away from her.

As the taxi turned from the paved public thoroughfare
onto the semi-private gravel road to Pine Grove Dwellings,
Nikki realized that her fighting spirit had lost much of it
zeal. Right away deciding that she needed to walk and revive
her resolve, she said to the driver, "Can we stop here,

please."

"Is only a li'l bit more, you know. Couple hundred meters 'round that curve," the man offered.

"Is nothing. I just want to walk a bit. You know how I mean?"

He shrugged and stopped the taxi.

"Thank you so much," she said, meeting his eyes, showing a neutral smile. She paid him and got out.

"Pleasure's mine," returned the hero. Then he engaged gears and drove on ahead of her around the curve and was gone.

The receding sound of the engine returned the surroundings to nature. A gentle breeze tickled the mischievous curl on her forehead and she let it be. Or perhaps she was too distracted by a sudden burst of spirited birdsong. Whatever else it might've been, that whistle was definitely some sort of signal, as it seemed all at once every other singing bird was trying to make itself heard. Chaotic din no doubt, but the bedlam was vivacious and provoked a smile.

Lighter of heart she strolled along, her canvas loafers crunching the graveled path, sounding a soothing cheer for every step she took. To her left the steep sober hills were covered with conifers, their trunks grayish, the forest's floor coated in a bright umber of fallen spines. To her right was a stand of old timber. Shafts of sunlight pierced the shadows between the great gnarled trunks, the sporadic cheeps and whistles of birds adding to an impression that it was cooler under there.

She rounded the curve to see an extensive open, sloping

area that used to be an orange plantation. It failed because clandestine slash-and-burn farmers depleted the ground vegetation that prevented soil erosion. The destruction only stopped when the government sold the land to developers; who then employed some of the same illegal farmers as security guards. A solution that suited everyone—new owners getting peace of mind, the former farmers making a 'food'—as in putting meals on the family table.

From Vivion's vague stories she gathered that his grandfather used connections in the Ministry of Agriculture & Land Affairs to own some twenty-five acres of this roughly crescent-shaped, slightly sloping plot of land in the southern foothills of the Northern range. He built the bungalow and they lived there as a family. Then years later after a trip to New York, his mother used some of her inheritance to set about building this multiplex of fifteen dwellings.

It was an open square of adjacent two-storied houses in three quintets set at right angles to each other. The backyards of each quintet extended into the surrounding forests of conifers planted by a concerned government to manage soil erosion on the sloping landscape. Each quintet of dwellings fronted a half-an-acre square which, at its middle, sported a copse of mango trees featuring two mango Rose, four mango Doux-Doux, and four ever-bearing, ever-green mango John.

Further up the hill of conifers, completing the picture like a cap over the impressive layout of Pine Grove Dwellings complex, was Nikki's destination. Fifty or so meters on, then up twenty broad flat concrete steps was

Missus Pinheiro's grand residence, or as the area folks had nicknamed it, the Bungalow.

When she got to the front of the property the sentry hut was empty and the driveway gate wide open. As she went through a voice asked, "Yes Miss. Can I help you?"

It was a lanky smiling fellow clad in Security khaki taking a smoke in the shade of the sentry hut.

"I'm going to see Missus Pinheiro."

"And your name?"

"Miss Grant-Ali," said Nikki as she fingered away the mischievous curl tickling her forehead.

The fellow straightened up from his recline against the hut and gave her a look sharp with reassessment. With forefinger and thumb he squeezed the cigarette out and put the butt carefully in his front shirt pocket. Then he opened a log book to a page and glanced at his watch and wrote. He asked, "Is Missus Pinheiro expecting you, Miss Grant-Ali?"

"No. But she'd want to see me."

"Well, thank you, Miss Grant-Ali. You can go on up." His hand reached towards his shirt pocket.

Nikki was unsettled when, halfway up the flat wide steps leading to the bungalow's front verandah, she saw a movement that turned out to be Missus Pinheiro—an imperious fifty-ish Creole with thick, curly, graying shoulder-length hair who sat prim and straight in an old fashioned rocking-chair that slowly moved back and forth on its rockers.

A bit darker than Nikki expected—Vivion being so light and his mother but two, three shades lighter than Nikki herself—except that her color was indefinite, somewhere between copper and olive. She was a busty woman with large hazel eyes in a smooth-skinned, diamond-shaped face. Her mouth was small with expressive lips, which at the moment, were pursed in disfavor. A folding fan in her right hand lazily shifting breezes, she had the airs of a confident empress taking her ease.

Startled to a stop, fighting spirit a-quiver, Nikki said, "Oh hello, Missus Pinheiro. Good morning. I didn't see you there."

No pause at all in her actions, eyes focused on baskets of hanging plants arranged around the verandah, Missus Pinheiro said, "That's all right. Is because I sitting so much higher than you."

Nikki continued to the top of the steps wondering if she had been taunted and said, "Oh, I'm Shanika—"

"I know who you is," interrupted Missus Pinheiro mildly, "I just wasn't expecting anybody."

Now Nikki was certain she was skipping rope on a razor's edge. Temper in check and choosing words carefully, she said, "I only come by because it urgent and I want to talk to you before I make any moves."

Missus Pinheiro stopped her rocking and fanning and looked at Nikki from under raised, skeptical eyebrows. "What so urgent? What moves?" she asked quietly.

Nikki fed worry into her voice and played her best card. "Well, Vivion gone and I don't know where. He only leave a note that don't say nothing."

To Nikki's consternation, Missus Pinheiro calmly resumed her rocking and fanning and showing interest in things other than Nikki. "Is only first time he do that?" she asked.

"Yes," said Nikki, meek now that her ace bomb turned out to be a dud that didn't even fizz.

Missus Pinheiro added nodding to her unconcern display as she focused on open space a meter to the left of Nikki. "So what you want me to do about all this, Miss Gran—"

The eye avoidance pose was the last straw. Temper slipping its reins, Nikki interrupted, "Look here, Missus Pinheiro! Don't play that with me. Okay! I mean, please don't. Not now. I know you don't like the situation between me and Vivion. But we can't work on that if you keep on cold-shouldering me. So call me Nikki, or even Shanika. But my name is not Miss anything. Not to you."

"Oh ho! So you don't prefer your formal family name?"

"Missus Pinheiro, you well know that's not what I mean. Look, I trying. I trying hard and you know it. What I prefer, what I want is to be, er, you know. Well at least yuh friend. I prefer and want you as a happy grandmother to mih children. I prefer and want that you to treat me like family. For in truth, I feel like that already and I like it and don't intend to stop."

"Is like you have a lot of preferences, eh girl," said Missus Pinheiro, but her tone was softer, her manner placating, even amused.

Encouraged, Nikki said, "Not really, Ma'am. I might want what I want. But in truth, I always been a sucker for peace over anything else."

Missus Pinheiro heaved a great sigh and—shorter than

her persona—stood up out of her rocking chair. "Let we go on the back porch," she said. "It cooler there from a breeze that coming down from the pines."

Through the front door that squeaked when opened, she led them into a large dim living-room that smelled faintly of cedar-wood, then through a hallway past a door to what had to be a kitchen, then past another closed door painted white that by its smaller size might've been a bathroom, then finally out onto the back verandah which now seemed to run all around the colonial style bungalow.

Missus Pinheiro indicated a pair of rocking-chairs placed side by side. "Have a seat, Nikki," she said, then raised her voice and called, "Ramiya! Ram—"

From within the house there came the sound of approaching footsteps and an exasperated voice: "Okay, okay! Stop deafening the damned doorposts!" Then a woman in a baggy, floral-patterned bathrobe came through the door. A full-fleshed woman colored that full-moon tinted gold of Taino people. Her wet hair was long, straight, black, and twisted into a loose braid that hung dripping over her shoulder. Her face, with high cheek bones, had flawless skin enlivened by black, wide set, slightly slanted upward eyes. Her snub nose flared over an expressive full-lipped mouth and a dimpled chin. Hers was a face a Gauguin would love. As she noticed Nikki she pulled close the robe's neck and instantly lost her impatient manner, saying, "Oh-oh! I didn't realize we had company. Was in the shower. But what you calling about?"

Missus Pinheiro said, "I didn't realize either. This is Nikki"—at which both the Ramiya and Nikki acknowledged each other with polite eyes and nods— "When you get time, would you be a dear and bring us some coconut water. It gone so hot out there in the front."

"No problem, Luz. Back in a jiffy," said Ramiya and went back inside.

At Nikki's questioning look, Missus Pinheiro smiled. "Yes, she calls me Luz. Short for Andaluza, my first name. She's my sister and lives here. She helped bring up Vivion. And no. You can't call me Luz. But you could call me Andaluza 'cause from you I won't like 'Mother' so much."

Deep but quietly Nikki breathed of relief and pleasure. She felt a flush rising in her neck and face; a surging, glowing spark of triumph that had her eyes filling. Needful to more fully express her feelings, she rushed over and knelt before Andaluza in her rocking chair and hid her head in the older woman's lap. She tried to say "Thank you so much" but got only to 'Thank' before she was sobbing her gratitude instead.

The mother in Andaluza Pinheiro patted Nikki's head and gently stroked her lustrous tresses. "Dear, dear," she murmured soothingly, "no. No tears. Happiness need smiles to thrive. Yuh hair really nice in truth, you know. I like how it curly and soft so."

They were still there sharing bonding understandings when Ramiya returned. She had changed into an all-white outfit—loose-fitting slacks and a roguish T-shirt that teased about the voluptuous body within. She was pushing a wheeled serving-tray loaded with three cold-sweating glasses, two bowls of furry ice cubes, a two-liter thermos flask of fresh coconut water, a bottle of Angostura bitters, a half glass of sparkling brown liquor, and a plate of hot cashew-nut cakes giving off a mouthwatering aroma. "All right ladies," she declared with a sarcastic smile. "Enough of all this emotional carrying on, okay! Leh we now celebrate true relations."

Which, after fixing beverages to their particular tastes, they did.

The lime broke up around three-thirty when Andaluza cried out, "O Lord Eshu, is almost four o'clock and I sitting here old-talking and laughing. Me, who have real business waiting." She stood up abruptly, slapped the lap of her skirt free of cake crumbs, looked at Nikki and said mock crossly, "Okay you! Miss Sweet-Talking-Story-Teller. From now on I watching you close. Okay! So you coming by me tomorrow after lunch to continue yuh fairy tales. You hear me. After lunch. Well after lunch." Then carrying herself erect, she marched off into the house.

On cue with Andaluza's exit, Ramiya's bellow of laughter waggled Nikki's consternation, shifting it into the realm of humor and relaxed her into smiling. "So this is Vivion's mother," she thought fondly.

Thus began a series of daily visits between the women—Nikki always going to the Bungalow, excepting Tuesday of that first week when they all went to the palace primarily to help bring back some of Nikki's painting materials. Then after a solitary walk checking out the garden and whatever, it was so close enough to sunset Andaluza decided they'd stay the night.

Nikki made dinner and afterwards, settled them in

upstairs with its two bedrooms with bathrooms. While, spicing her dreams with his faded scent, she slept in Vivion's king-size bed.

Next morning as they waited for the taxi, Ramiya confessed that she'd always wanted to get a *feel* of her boy's palace—the 'her boy' part setting Nikki's gossip wheels a-wondering.

ooOoo

FROM THE AIRPORT, VIVION took the express bus to
Manhattan then the A train to West Seventy-Eight street.
His heading was a modest hostel near Central Park where he
always stayed when in New York. The business was owned
by an older straight-backed Jewess who sat on a steel
rocking chair; a throne from which she made snarky
comments about what went on. A dark-skinned middle-aged
Jamaican man, Rawlston John, actually checked in the
guests. A chatty fellow quick to brag about the outstanding
prowess of Caribbean athletes, he hit it off with Vivion and,
first visit, suggested that in bygone times he and the woman
had had a romantic relationship based on his sprinting
ability.

Neither one was present when Vivion got there. A
bright-eyed young college type paused his computer's action
and checked him in.

Suggested by a girlfriend who had stayed there, Vivion
considered this hostel safe and convenient, ideal for his

temporary needs. Thirty dollars a night—twenty-five if you stayed three weekends—bought him a room with a comfortable single bed covered by two flannel sheets and a yielding pillow, a chair tucked under a tray-sized desk, a sink for a cold water faucet, and a small radio. Cozy was a nice word for it. In the hall, two common bathrooms with showers serviced eight rooms on the sixth floor. There was a pay phone here, too, and free internet access in the office downstairs.

Vivion took a room facing the street and slept the rest of that night with the window open and the blinds pulled down. After the monotonous drone of the airplane, nighttime traffic sounds were soothing.

He spent Monday morning checking over appointments made by email two days before he left. He read over his pepper materials, refined his sales pitch. Then sometime after noon, feeling peckish, he went out and, attracted by the delicious aromas, followed his nose to a hot bread-and-scrambled-meat sandwich from a street vendor sporting a thick, trimmed, black moustache. Vivion stood in the stand's shadow and devoured the tasty food, helped it down with a bottle of unnaturally yellow orange juice. When done, he praised the meal, at which the vendor broke out a broad white smile and said, "Praise and thanks to Allah, my friend."

"Amen to that," said Vivion. "You stay nice!"

He started back to the hostel, but it being such a pippin of a day, decided instead to take a little jaunt. To re-familiarize himself was his weak excuse, and anyway, he knew his business stuff by heart. So he headed to Central

Park and spent the afternoon pleasurably roaming, going nowhere.

Dressed in his business outfit, in sunny mood and determined to succeed, Vivion exited the subway at 34th street and walked east to the address in his pocket notebook. The building was a refurbished warehouse from an earlier age, still with an old-time freight elevator, albeit renovated to automatic. His palms were sweating when he pressed the button to the seventh floor. He made a smug grimace with his mouth and nodded, feeling right and ready for any. He got out the elevator and strode along a hallway of offices with numbers displayed on frosted glass doors. He turned right twice before coming upon # 738 with the inscription in bold, black, and large calligraphy that proclaimed:

LAMBKIN   &   HARRIS—IMPORTS   AND EXPORTS.

He pressed the buzzer, heard it respond inside, and waited a longish minute before the door cracked open a foot or so. From behind it came an unhappy male voice that should've been trying for hearty but only managed a peevish, "Come on in."

Amused, Vivion crab-walked through the narrow opportunity into a small ante-office. An obvious secretary's area, it featured a suitably small desk dominated by a desktop computer and the regulation black office phone with a print-out pad of numbers on its right-hand side.

While Vivion's gaze roamed he felt the fellow giving him a quick look over as he said, "Follow me, please."

The fellow was of middle height and thin. Like an axe blade, his face narrowed as it came towards the nose, which itself used hardly any space at all. At barely past ten o'clock, already he had sprouted black fuzz on cheeks and chin and neck—this was a man would always need a shave. His black trousers were crumpled, and the long-sleeved white shirt carelessly tucked into his belted waist was unbuttoned at the sweat-stained collar. At his neck a thin, loosened, black tie adorned the open-necked shirt.

Vivion followed him four, five steps to another frosted glass door that showed the identical inscription as that of the front door. The fellow opened the door and invited again, "Come in."

This time Vivion saw a smile that still needed work and realized that the guy was trying hard as, with a hand gesture, he indicated the chair on the visitor side of an imposing desk and said, "Please have a seat."

Vivion sat in the black chair so heavy it might've been made of marble. It came with dark brown leather trimmings. A cool back rest. Arm rests that were just the right height for the elbows, and soft all the way around. A seductive seat that'd comfort grateful gluteals.

The fellow went to the big glass window and adjusted the shades, barring some happy sunbeams from the striking desk. Mostly because it was a rich dark brown, Vivion guessed mahogany, but whatever its roots, with all its edges and corners smooth and rounded, and all the room underneath when Vivion stretched his long legs, it was indeed an impressive piece of craftsmanship.

Just before he sat, the guy stuck out a hand and said,

"I'm David Lambkin, at your service. Forgive the delay to the door. I forgot my secretary is out."

Vivion shook the damp hand, said, "Pleased. I'm Vivion Pinheiro," and sat.

As David Lambkin took his seat behind the grand polished desk and almost disappeared, Vivion noticed a faint, unpleasant smell, like spilled stale beer. He shifted attention to the big shaded window while, peripherally, he saw pale blue eyes glancing at him, never focusing, but straying about the room as if eluding confrontation.

Then David Lambkin pulled a file close, opened it and as his finger scrolled down, offered, "And you are here for—?"

"Peppers. Selling peppers," Vivion supplied.

"Oh!" said David Lambkin absently, as if the datum filled no gaps in his comprehension.

Vivion reminded, "We set up this appointment a week ago, by email and then phone. I might have spoken to you, or your partner. I'm not good with accents. But here I am, ready and willing to discuss peppers. Very hot peppers from Trinidad. In fact, the hottest in the world! I'm here to talk about my current production, about you importing it and introducing it to the American market. I believe that you folks are ready for the best." He ended by baring his charming smile. The gleaming teeth. Extra crinkle at the eyes.

"Trinidad, Trinidad," David Lambkin stared at Vivion as he mused aloud. "Moruga Red Scorpion. Not so?" he asked.

"Exactly so!" enthused Vivion. At last he was getting

somewhere.

"You Portuguese?" asked David Lambkin.

Upon which Vivion got that warm discomfort in his chest that turned on sweat glands in his palms. An undermining feeling he had known since elementary school. The isolated sensation he always had when talk turned to his origins, about who was his father. So he hid an instant disappointment that he wouldn't be working with David Lambkin, an importer more interested in ancestry than hot peppers.

From behind a deprecatory smile he said, "Nah, man. In Trinidad, where I from, we have all kinda races and ethnicities. We're a mixture of every heritage, every people on the planet. Is one of the things we famous for."

"But yours is originally a Portuguese name. Not so?" Lambkin persisted.

In a valiant effort not to be rude, Vivion said, "Well, Mr. Lambkin, I really don't know, you know. For example, we have Lambkins in Trinidad some of them black like La Brea tar. Some of them whiter than you. Where I come from there's not much originality to a name. Is because of inter-breeding. You know, racial intermingling and so forth. But what you say we talk peppers, eh? I exporting, you importing and passing on to a hungry American market. What you say?"

David Lambkin's face sort of squeezed tighter on itself and his hands went busy. The left opened a near drawer on its side, reached briefly into it, then gently pushed it in to close with a soft sucking sound. Then David Lambkin leaned himself over to his right and pulled open a drawer, but changed his mind and slid it shut. Instead, he drew the appointments folder closer to him, bit his under lip as he studied its content. Then the phone rang and he halfway rose from his seat and reached across the desk to pick it up and repeat "Yes" and "I get it" like a junior partner when he wasn't intently listening.

All while Vivion mentally pumped a victorious fist—having from the first decided that the swanky desk was much too much for puny David Lambkin. More than just stature, he'd have to grow a lot to suit it.

The rest of the meeting was a meaningless back and forth of empty promises and, as the wet stains at David Lambkin's armpits enlarged, Vivion realized that the wafting stale-beer odor was the man's anxiety scent.

His eyes returned to roving, Lambkin mouthed about complications and due dates and difficulties but was willing to give it a go depending on due diligence and demands of the coming season.

Vivion murmured his understanding and willingness to be patient. He, too, would await more perfect circumstances.

Lambkin gave Vivion a card with his data: email; phones, office and cell; the office's street address.

Vivion wrote his less used email address and his Magic Jack number on the desk's scratch pad.

Then they shared a quick, damp handshake at the inner frosted door as Vivion said, "So take care now. I'll let myself out."

The relief in David Lambkin's "Goodbye" was assurance that they'd never again meet.

During workdays of the next two weeks Vivion kept ten of a dozen appointments he had made by email or phone from Trinidad. After meeting a fourth associate manager Vivion patched together a basic manager profile based on office location and furnishings, and the men's manner and body language. He also bet himself that future others would be similarly underlings without authority, and useless to his purpose.

One office he visited had a sign on its opaque glass door that recommended "Ring the bell and enter!"

Vivion did.

At which an overweight man shot up from his desk and stared at Vivion as if he'd materialized out of the disinfectant scent in the air. "I'm Simmons," he said and stuck out his hand.

It was the swiftest, slipperiest handshake Vivion ever experienced as he said, "I'm Vivion Pinheiro, the pepper guy from Trini—"

"I was expecting a girl, er, I mean a woman," Simmons interrupted. "Vivian, you know?"

Vivion's deliberate shrug was elaborate. Politely dismissive more than reassuring. "Yeah, man," he said, as Simmons pulled a handkerchief from his jacket pocket and began mopping sudden sweat springing from his balding head and face.

This initial awkwardness insurmountable, pepper-wise, the rest of their business was short and fruitless.

Another day it was a fellow whose heavy belly was at hard effort contesting the embrace of a blue-striped white cotton shirt. Given the task of containing the bulging mass, the garment had ordered its lower buttons to give the universal upside down 'V' surrender sign. The man above though, didn't seem to care about these ongoing tensions. A round-faced fellow with a broad, big-toothed smile, he held a cigar that diffused thin blue sinuous smoke into the air. He had a hearty manner with voice to suit. "Have a seat," he invited with a sweeping gesture. "I'm Bobby Nance. Yes, have a seat, my friend," he offered again, "make yourself comfy. Then tell me what I can do you for?"

Vivion's glances bounced around the space: from the large desk that commanded most of the small room, to the five-paneled window that opened onto an orderly brick wall, then to the small table at which an inconspicuous woman crouched—a table with barely top enough for the computer and the office phone that occupied it.

He sat down in the plain straight-backed chair indicated and made a halfhearted pitch while a large part of his mind strayed to wondering how the nondescript woman in the far corner of the room survived this poisonous attack on her lungs.

He said the proper things and left that smoke-filled space as soon as it was politely possible.

Other men he met varied in body shape, and age, and quantity of hair on big or narrow or nice-shaped heads. Some wore eyeglasses, some did not. He couldn't be certain, but surnames inscribed on their opaque-glass office doors were mostly different.

The coincidence of two companies being in the same ugly warehouse-style building only allowed him to win his waste-of-time wager with himself sooner, as day after frustrating day, nothing positive resulted from the meetings.

He missed two appointments when he got lost in the subway system and ended up in Brooklyn rather than Queens. But by then, Thursday afternoon of the second week, he was so discouraged he never even called to apologize and/or reschedule.

The advert on a newspaper left on the subway seat screamed in large red type about a pre-Labor Day sale at Macy's. One of the boxed panels showed some nice sneakers going at half price. Always on the alert for comfortable footwear for his size thirteen's wide, he took himself over for a look see.

He was on the street floor near the front of a crowd waiting for elevators that seemed stuck on the third. All four of them were, and shoppers had become impatient. Someone male back of the crowd opined, "Dey does only give dese sales to tantalize people, *oui*." It was a Trinidadian voice and the comment rang true to the spirit of that culture. Vivion glanced back but couldn't see the speaker.

The wait for the elevator continued.

Trini-man next observed that the escalator too, was not moving. "Like something happen on dat third floor, yu'know," he said.

That catalyzed some movements among the waiting crowd. Several people with other things to do wormed out of the press and went away.

Then Trini-man again: "Is like dey have we trap, *oui*. Offering half price and no road to de bargains. I say dey just playing with we. Is just *mamaguy*."

Vivion looked back again and this time got a glimpse of the fellow, and thought he recognized him. Enough to make up his mind that he would wait no longer, and instead, check out this fellow who looked familiar. He squeezed through more patient shoppers, headed towards the Trini fellow and saw him face to face and realized that it was Mervyn Charles, a guy who, back home, occasionally limed on Vivion's crew's bench. Grown a little heavier in cheeks and chest, a few white streaks in his hair, but definitely Mervyn Charles.

Vivion called, "Mervyn Charles, is you dey?"

Mervyn looked his way, said, "Hey, Reds Pinheiro. Wha' you doing here, man?"

And that was it. Right away Mervyn was off on how commerce in the City was on a moral downswing. Trust was a lost virtue. A used-to-be quality. The king called Craft had been overthrown. Shoddy products of planned obsolescence in attractive packaging now ruled. Merchants saw customers as consumers in an equation where consuming lowered folks to the bottom of Commerce Kingdom hierarchy.

Vivion halfway listening, sported a fond smile that admired how the older fellow had remained true to himself—a political, philosophical, gossipy Voice of One.

Out of the store, shopping intentions abandoned, Mervyn led them to a softly lit, nice slightly tobacco-smelling bar, and nursing three over-priced beers they chatted for an hour catching up on past times, remembered people, places, and events. Being strictly an Old Oak man, Vivion had only one brew while Mervyn brought him up to date about other fellows from their lime who had emigrated. He appreciated the irony. Here he was, on a brief trip from home, getting stories from Mervyn about homeboys who had left so long ago.

He got the insides about how Garnet Conrad had made his girlfriend, Claudine Dodd, pregnant and had to marry. Then they went Toronto to live with his older brother David's people.

He found out that Nazir Mohammed's parents' house burned down from an electrical short and he had to leave high school and go work for the sugarcane factory until he was nineteen before he saved enough to move to Mumbai to study Islamic music.

He heard how Terry Clarke Langston accepted a track scholarship to Grambling University and was off to it like a flash.

That story triggered Mervyn to ask, "You remember Bobby Ting father?"

Vivion shook his head, "I not—"

Mervyn cut him off, "Man, you must. He had a grocery store by the school corner, opposite the gas station. We used to call him 'Mr. Obey-The-Highway-Code.'"

"Ah-ha, yes! I remember Mr. Highway-Code. A Chinese fella. Used to wear Gandhi glasses."

"That's the man! Well them glasses didn't help in the long run. He died in a three-car pile up on Solomon Hochoy highway and it send his wife crazy. So she brother take she to live with them, and Bobby and he two sisters had to manage the store. Well they turn out to be a great team and soon, three years max, they did well enough for the girls to leave for schooling in England. One doing law, one economics. Then, a few months after that went down, Bobby sell the grocery and move up here to Queens. He pay down on a brownstone and next thing you hear he frenning with a chubby li'l mix-breed named Halima Leema. They had met some years before in the Poly-Tech. They must still have something sweet going on because in the last few years he father three children, first identical twin boys, then a girl. While all that happening, Halima convert their downstairs into a thriving roti shop. The menu have Dahlpuree, Plain, Skins, Buss-up-Shot, Doubles, anything you want. She even selling small roti with pockets you could fill up with yuh own choice. You know, like Richard's Bake and Shark in Maracas Bay."

"Chinese and Indian, them children must look good," said Vivion.

"Probably. Is a nice blend. I never seen these particular ones, but they remind me of Roopnarinesingh. You remember him?"

"Nah," said Vivion.

Mervyn sucked his teeth in mild exasperation, said, "Where you been, Reds? You never hear 'bout Roop, the Mighty Roop? A dark-skinned Chinese-looking young fella who try singing calypso for a season until he stage name break him down. Roop does sound too much like Foops, and you know how them calypsonians wicked when it come to *picong*. The poor boy just couldn't stand the jibes.

Everybody making fart jokes about him, so he drop out and end up running a tour boat business in Buccoo Reef. Making good money, too. I telling you, calypso singing ent for everybody!"

Vivion chuckled and nodded, sipped warm beer.

Mervyn took a sip himself and said, "Talking about Chinese. You was tight with Spoon, not so?"

Spoon was J. Harry 'Spoonface' Douglas, one of Vivion's best buddies during those precious gilt-edged teenage days. "Yeah, man," said he, "was a time when Spoonface was mih main man. Then when I was in UWI he went up North."

"You right, he immigrate to back-up Trinidad, which is Brooklyn, New York," said Mervyn with a grin.

"Americans make that official yet?"

"Only on Labor Day," laughed Mervyn as he took out his cell phone and copied down Spoon's number, street address, and subway directions on a paper napkin and handed it to Vivion. "So this is he details if you want to see him. Yes, man, Spoon settle down nice-nice. He living in Brooklyn close to six years now. I ent have details, but I hear that the woman he marry is fine and wealthy and a naturalized American. Hong Kong Chinese, I think. I know that they have two children. Though it might even be three. I ent sure which . . ."

As he listened with one ear, Vivion was wondering how Mervyn gathered all this data. A gentle smile tugged at his lips as he remembered Mervyn being always that way—a gregarious fellow, nice with everybody. The person you'd least mind gossiping your business—not at all like Mr.

Observe-from-the-sidelines Vivion, himself.

When Mervyn had exhausted his news, best as he could, Vivion passed on the latest that he knew of mutual friends still in Trinidad. Though in truth, it was not really much, or as interesting. Still they had a good lime and before parting shared phone numbers and street addresses—Vivion giving up the Magic Jack number he had back home. Even promised to run by Mervyn's place, although he knew this was unlikely as he had so many business matters to take care of in the remaining week.

Vivion got off the train at Times Square and decided to walk to the hostel. As he strolled along he got to ruminating about his friend of whom, and from whom he hadn't heard, far less seen, for donkey's years—hadn't even suspected he was in New York.

Mervyn's stories about Spoon were no surprise—they fitted snugly with the fella Vivion knew. It was due to J. Harry's good looks and natural talents that crew and closest named him Spoon-face. That his skin was smooth as a silver spoonful of creamy chocolate only supported the appropriateness of the nickname. Spoon didn't only have charm, though. He was also smart and lucky and lazy in exactly effective measures. And allowing for minor alterations of a few features, Spoon had realized the most satisfying dream of every fellow in their lime back then—before they found out or followed their particular mature paths.

When Vivion got to his room he showered, then went out to a Spanish restaurant around the corner. He ordered a *pollos y arroz rojo* dinner to go. He'd eat it in the hostel because for him, after the lime with Mervyn, it was the homiest food available.

Then anticipating the visit to his long lost buddy, he went to sleep early.

ooOoo

AFTER THEIR TUESDAY NIGHT stay at the Palace, Andaluza said she'd be busy mornings and that Nikki should visit in the afternoons when she'd be home.

When, as usual, Nikki awoke around ten this bright Saturday morning, she decided to visit Andaluza and share with her the cool pleasant day. Furthermore, the light was perfect for what she had in mind for the portrait she was making. Usually halfway through a painting she'd get a need for reality. Camera shots were helpful for remembering, but nothing beats the actual scene for the way light lived on skin and gave it color and vibrancy.

So she checked her emails, had a shower, made and ate breakfast. Then she called Mr. Dylan for a taxi to Pine Grove Dwellings. Nikki was dressed and ready at ten forty-five when she heard the car horn toot at the yard gate. She picked up her handbag, locked the house and was out of there.

An Indian woman in a crisp white-shirt-black-slacks

chauffeur's uniform stood aside the passenger's door. Surprised, Nikki said, "You know this is first time I get a female driver." The driver open the door and Nikki got into the car.

The driver was young, close either side of twenty and about five foot four. She had a heart-shaped face with a pert nose and a wide mouth that smiled neat white teeth. Her smiles came easy and quick. Large dark pupils in light brown eyes gave a suggestion of boldness, and an abundance of pitch-black hair, straight and glossy, and flung careless about the epaulette of her white shirt buttressed that fancy. "Yeah," she said, "Mr. Dylan trying to give woman a chance. Some female passengers prefer to have a female driver anyhow. You know, they feel safer."

"Is a great idea. Some male drivers think every woman in their car looking for man."

"You telling I?" agreed the driver. "If you want you could ask for me next time. I is Aaqilah, the oldest Madani child. We have a bakery up by the Dial, but when school on holidays I does pull some bull, make some money."

"Which school you going?"

"UT&T. I doing Info and Communications Tech," said Aaqilah Madani.

Impressed by the ambitious young woman, Nikki asked, "How much longer you have?"

"A year and a half, or maybe two, once I could make tuition. In any case I could get good part-times after I finish next year courses."

"Well, good luck, girl. I like how you moving. You spell Aaqilah with two a's or one?" asked Nikki, saying the name from back of her throat, Arabic fashion, as she took her notebook from her handbag.

Aaqilah flashed a glance back at Nikki as she said, "Two," then asked, "You Muslim?"

"Yes. Why?"

"Well, is how you say mih name the glottic way, back of yuh throat and all," she chuckled, self-deprecating, continued, "then is yuh long curly hair and yuh color. I woulda say you is a Dougla."

"I *is* a Dougla. Mih father is a Indian imam. Mih mother mixed-up Creole, African with the usual others."

"That explain it. Typical Trini callaloo, eh," laughed Aaqilah. "Is what does bring out the prettiness in we!"

Nikki said, "Well, thank you!" and settled back thoughtful in the taxi. She had bought their famous cornbread from Madani bakery, had been served by a skinny impatient man, probably this girl's father who now, for Nikki, had grown enormous in stature. Mr. Madani had transformed into a Muslim father hopeful and loving enough to name his female firstborn the Arabic word for 'intelligent'.

Nikki herself was a first child, and according to her mother, her father, a prominent imam at the time, had no female name prepared for his newborn. Mammy, in a state of post-partum euphoria, was unreachable for opinion. So as he left the hospital room, Babu okayed her to be named after the Afro-Trini midwife who delivered her.

Not that Nikki even minded the name Shanika, but Mr. Madani's bold foresight impressed, and gradually the notion of a scholarship for straight-talking, ambitious, hard-working young women formed her mind.

When Nikki got to the bungalow Ramiya answered her call at the front door; something she hardly did. Fearing the worse, Nikki said, "Don't tell me Andaluza gone out."

Ramiya was curt, "Well she *did* tell you she was busy mornings."

"But is a weekend," protested Nikki.

Ramiya put her hands on her ample hips and looked hard at Nikki. "So that mean what? Wind stop blowing weekend? Money stop spending weekends? The world stop spinning—"

"Okay, okay, okay," Nikki cut in. "I get the picture. But why you so cross with me? What I do you?"

"I ent vexed with nobody, nuh," said Ramiya as she turned and flounced off into the house.

Nikki followed into the kitchen and saw that Ramiya had been disturbed from kneading bread dough. "Bread or fry bake?" she asked.

Ramiya pursed her lips and twisted them downwards. She tossed her head unhappily, said, "It was to be coconut bread. But them vendors so blasted undependable. You'd think that since I put in a order two days now I would get mih goods in time, eh. You would think, not so?"

Now Nikki felt better as she realized why Ramiya was vexed. "Don't take it on, girl. These people will drive you crazy. In any case I like anything you make, so if you unhappy with the plain bread I will take it off your hands. That's only if you want me to 'cause I don't want to muddy waters with anybody . . . " She left the statement hanging open-ended.

Ramiya caught the hint and was chuckling. "Child, don't let my bad mood spoil your good one, okay," she said, grinning camaraderie. "I think is mih hormones acting up."

"Them damned hormones. Can't live with them, can't live without them" said Nikki, her grin as broad.

An hour later, bread baked, spread with guava jam, then sampled and judged satisfactory, they were on the back terrace, chatting. Ramiya was seated in a bentwood high-chair sipping from a half tumbler of brandy while, fan brush in hand and straddling a three-legged stool, Nikki was behind her easel musing aloud about Vivion's palace: "Ramiya, I serious. I think he could make that house a showcase. A sort of conservation platform for how to save the planet. Stop climate change and global warming. You know what I mean? They'd feature it in the newspapers as ultra-modern. The coming thing in house architecture. You see what I saying?"

"Is a good idea. And I smiling because is like Vivion infecting you with he wild schemes. Listen girl, that boy, he don't stick to any single project. Once he solve one he moving on. Yes, he could help save the world but I bet you he'd never take it on."

"Why not? He certainly like bragging 'bout he self-sufficient palace."

"He might brag to you and maybe me and he mother. But in the heart a' him, that boy too bashful. He never will call that much attention on he-self."

"Vivion! Bashful! That's not what I see in him."

"You ent know him long enough, child. That's all. But in time you going find out."

"Ramiya, you making me nervous how you saying that."

"Don't be, girl," Ramiya said. "Vivion is a good boy. He stick to what he like," she paused to make four eyes with Nikki before continuing, "and in the present case, I could say who that is. Girl! Your Vivion have better ways than most. Who don't know him close will never see he true depth. He good at hiding it behind a cool could-care-less mask. Listen me close and I'll tell you a little story before Luz get back." She sipped of her brandy and continued, "I suppose you know that when he was doing University studies Luz bought him a piece of property that used to be a cocoa estate."

"Yeah," said Nikki, "he tell me something 'bout that. But I does get caught up listening to the voice instead of what he saying. That ever happen to you?"

"Nikki darling, I not young and in love, okay. But anyhow, about the land. Buying it was he mammy business instinct making moves, and if you have to understand Andaluza Pinheiro at all, you have to realize that bottom line, she is a businesswoman. A clever one who would bargain with who ever devil, and always, well, usually get what she want. Don't let she size fool you. I say she get that instinct from she father, Señor Eduardo, and he was a old-fashioned colonist living high up on the mountain of white-man privilege."

Ramiya stopped to clear her throat and wipe her face—perhaps her eyes too—Nikki couldn't be certain. Although the woman's voice had cracked emotional when she spoke of Andaluza's father.

"But you didn't ask so I not saying. But getting back to how that purchase come about. You should know that the year Vivion went University, nothing to keep she attention, Luz decided to accept invitation and visit a cousin through she father sister who was living in New York. She name was Sierra Pinheiro de Soto as she did marry a fella from Argentina and had a child with him. They name the child Dahomey. Yes, Dahomey de Soto. The family joke was that Sierra, named after a mountain, name her girl-child after a country that change name. Funny, eh?"

"What's the new name?" Nikki asked.

"Benin, or something like that," said Ramiya. "But I can't see why they make the change. The new name not as nice as Dahomey."

"O Benin! I hear 'bout. Is a tourist destination if you interested in obeah," said Nikki.

"Yeah that could be true. All voodoo and obeah and capoiera start in Dahomey. But back to Sierra, I can't rightly recall the Argentine fella, she husband first name. Maybe Bernard, or something so. But they had done well in the real estate racket and by the time Luz visit—that's what, eight, nine years gone now? By that time Sierra, by she self, own three or four two-bedroom houses that she was renting to newlyweds on two-year contracts. Another thing, by that time too, Sierra and the Latin husband had divorced and she was living with, and pregnant by, a brown-skinned American, a public school teacher named Darryl Jonas Jackson.

"Luz say he was a nice well-spoken fella and she liked

he name. But other than that, he was too dark for she own tastes. Nikki, one thing you should know. She funny that way, but you apart, Luz don't too like dark skin.

"But it was the real estate venture that impress she. She could see something like that extending she own real estate business. With how money was flowing from we country oil and gas fields, young people families was looking for better living spaces. You know, with a little lawn in the front yard, chickens in the back. A family starter sort a' place.

"Luz was thinking to build them decent enough but not fancy as she Pine Grove Dwellings," said Ramiya, then yawned and forcefully stretched her arms backwards. She looked at Nikki with a smile that made gleaming slits of her eyes, said, "Well, in for a penny, in for a pound," and took a long sip of her brandy before continuing.

"Well it was 'bout two, three months after Luz return from New York that she hear of the cocoa estate's misfortune and, using she father connections, was in the first row a' bidders when the property get auction off. She buy the top limit per bidder, twenty acres, and sign the common agreement that she going use the land for private and agricultural purposes.

"Back of she mind though, the only thing Luz intending to grow was profit.

"She looking at the property and seeing how she could divide up three or four acres into one lot plots, each with a modern two-bedroom cottage. She calling them cottage because it sound more high-class. So counting up, that making it six cottages every acre. About twenty families paying middle-class rent. All in all, a reliable fortune that, once it set up, didn't require much management.

"That the land was not yet designated for residential use was not a problem. The government minister in charge of that process was named Edward Baboolal. El Señor, Luz father Eduardo was he godfather. All it would take to reclassify it right was a visit to curry a favor. No big deal. Remember this was the twenty noughts. *Bobol* was alive and thriving all over the land.

"So one month after graduation, still bubbling with pride that he had done well, Luz enter she father den, the mahogany backroom that since a li'l boy, Vivion claim as he studying room. So Luz enter and present the money-mill proposal to she one-and-only.

"Well, girl, I don't have to describe the pain in she eyes as Luz telling me this thing. Because if you talking 'bout slight, Mr. Vivion Pinheiro never even look up from what ever he was doing on he grandfather mahogany desk. Never meet he mother eyes as he say that the whole scheme make him feel like a Scrooge. Say how the idea didn't matter anyhow since he, himself, had intentions for the land. Intentions!

"Then finally he turn full face and eyes square with she own, remind he mother that after all, the land was bought for him, in he name, and he was its sole owner now that he was twenty-one."

Ramiya sniffed syrupy snot up her nostrils and backhanded the tears wetting her cheeks. Took a swallow from her glass.

Nikki, herself choking up, looked at the older woman and understood why she and Andaluza were really the truest of siblings— sisters with feelings enough for each other they shed them as hot tears. Surprising herself, she reached over, took Ramiya's glass saying, "I need to clear mih throat."

"You see! The pagan in you coming out," goaded Ramiya.

"Nah! Not really. This going sound strange, but I want to know this other side of Vivion. Because to me, he's all sweetness and light—"

"Except like now when he gone off, eh?" Ramiya reminded, sarcasm weighing down her voice to a baritone.

Nikki shrugged, focused a chary eye on Ramiya, and challenged, "Well, you going to continue the story or what!"

Ramiya rolled her eyes upwards and sipped her brandy, said, "Well, where was I?"

"You was talking about when he declare he was the sole owner . . ."

"Yes, that's right. Well, girl, more painful than a *fer-de-lance* fang, them words hurt Andaluza. They crash on she soul like earthquake boulders. Confusion nearly break she will. Nikki! You have to understand that all the early years of we life together, Vivion had been he mother backup buddy, she chief booster. A dependable supporting shoulder. He was she reason for living with force and direction. So now this kinda coldness make she feel like she lose that steady rock. And right away she start thinking how he come back from the confounded University serious and judgmental to a fault, and definitely without they natural back-and-forth humor. She seeing all this as a trick meaning to annoy or make she out as a jackass.

"Late that night as she wetting mih shoulder with

distress, she complain about how it had become. Of late he was always with a 'Mother, look at the other side through their glasses!' or a 'Mother, walk a mile in their boots!' As if he was talking to an infant. Yes, a boring Mr. Tolerant-fair-minded-know-it-all! Like some kinda educated monster, that is who she one-and-only had turn into.

"Another thing was how he would make he soft voice harsh in a kinda chiding way and rake she feelings. But in she father study that sad Tuesday evening, Luz make she tears fall inward, out of she heart to bleed like a sigh into she soul. She hold head high, act like she didn't give a damn and went in she room. She close the door, turn the key, then loosen she hair and brush it until she arm aching. Then she come over by me, guzzle a half-glass a' mih brandy and lay she self down to sleep and gather and repair what was shattered."

While she was speaking, as the passion got to her Ramiya off and on shifted to the edge of her chair, tipping it forward as it did right then, taking Nikki's eyes from the canvas to lock with Ramiya's, which were again spilling quick tears, making bold tracks down to meet and drip from her trembling, defiant chin.

Touched to her core, Nikki reached over and with the back of her forefinger, wiped at the stream. Only interrupted it as Ramiya sipped from her brandy and continued, "Nikki! You know how they have it to say, 'Only woman does bleed!' Well, I is woman, and I telling you that the strongest woman does also cry. Pain and crying is part of they menu. But don't you ever feel that blood and tears sameway salty. Definitely not to a baby. A mother is a different kinda woman and she have a special kinda flow. A righteous mother does bleed milk of human kindness into she babies. From she teats into their minds she feeding fledglings to prepare them for a major challenge. A flight called living well. Successful mothers supply their offspring with safeguards. Securities of confidence that make them feel they is somebody. That's the kinda thing that turn a child in to the woman, and yes! fair is fair, or the man they going to be.

"So when you meet up them woman who try and fail that basic female test of being a mother. Well, you must feel sorry for them. They must be shame inside and hurting bad. Sometimes the best consolation they get is when they see even successful mothers having to learn how to manage disappointment."

Nikki had a sense that the talk about failed motherhood was intimate, and all at once unwilling to know more, said, "Ramiya, hear me now. You have to stop these heartbreak stories. All them tears ruining your face. Making mih nose stuff up so I can't think of what I do—"

"So now snot in yuh nose is yuh thinking thoughts?" Ramiya cut in, bursting out her great laugh, which despite their tear-stained faces, altogether altered the ambiance.

Minutes later, when the front door squeaked open, they winked at each other like conspirators and smiled as they switched the chat to commentary about the pleasant weather while Nikki aimlessly brush-stroked the canvas.

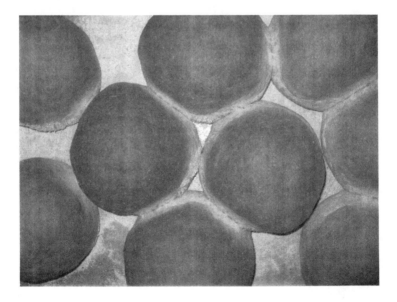

Bread Loaves

ooOoo

PEPPER BUSINESS PREDOMINANT in his mind, Vivion approached each day out among the New York natives aiming for modest, but effective, self-promotion. This Saturday morning, he put his backpack on the bed, unzipped it and absently scratching his scruffy twelve-day beard, considered the options of his spare wardrobe. As this visit was to a friend, the comfort of his old black Converse sneakers was a given; his only other footwear was a pair of black Clark's leathers for business events. Loose fitting and black, as well, he chose the jeans next.

Now came the self-promotion aspect of the outfit. He picked an off-white polo shirt with a discreet, volley-ball size logo on the right side chest—a red sphere in which, in black and red ink and bold font, was printed a semi-circular legend stating "PINHEIRO'S PEPPERS" in hot red, and below that, along the diameter, "ALMOST THE BEST" in skinny black. Then embracing the bottom curve of the sphere, "IN THE WORLD!" in vigorous scarlet.

Vivion had designed it himself and live-in lover and un-appointed business partner Nikki had approved. Which, she being a trained artist and portrait painter, sort of stamped it as guaranteed good enough.

Half an hour later, showered, dressed, looking and feeling smart, he was on his way. The Saturday morning he walked to the subway was precisely between pleasant and perfect; in the sixties, sunny, a gentle breeze bearing a slight scent of the public park's newly mowed grass. A promising late summer's day. He swiped his metro-card and was through the turnstiles, then short minutes later the train rumbled in. He boarded and was on his way to Brooklyn to connect with his longtime Trini partner, Junior Harold 'Spoonface' Douglas.

He was thinking about nothing in particular, gazing at advertising panels facing him when all at once Vivion realized that the guy seated opposite to him was staring at him. Immediately also, Intuition suggested that the fellow had been at it for a while!

Vivion collected himself, focused his eyes just left of the man's head as he gave the fellow a peripheral once over—a skinny youngish Asian wearing a light gray cotton jacket over a white T-shirt. Black pants that could've been linen. Soft black laced-up moccasins. A big-faced watch with many functions. The ensemble casually stylish and most likely expensive.

The directness of the man's stare suggested 'tourist' and was not intimidating. Since posting his self-sustaining house and the pepper farm operation in the official 'Things to do in Trinidad' brochure, Vivion had experienced a fair number of curious visitors to his gardens—they taking pictures of the house, asking questions about pepper varieties and propagation methods and so on. So all this in mind, he deliberately met the fellow's eye.

The fellow smiled and nodded his head sharply, Japanese style. Vivion smiled and barely stopping himself from mimicking, said "How you doing."

This time the fellow's returned nod was nearer to a bow as he said, "Very well, thank you." Then he pointed to Vivion's chest and said, "I am noticing your . . . " he made a circle in the air with his finger, ". . . advert?"

A zing of pride shot through his being as with a broad smile Vivion said, "Thank you so much. Yes sir, pepper is mih business."

"Very good. Very good. Me too. Pepper is the business, yes."

"Really?"

"Yes, yes. It is so," said the fellow, smiling and nodding vigorous emphasis. Then he left his seat, crossed the aisle to sit next to Vivion and stuck his hand out.

Vivion grasped the warm hand loosely and shook it, saying, "I'm Vivion Pinheiro from Trinidad. I export peppers. Hot peppers for spicy sauce."

"I am Hideo Arata, of Kumamoto City in Kyushu. I grow specialty peppers for family restaurant."

"Small world, my man. Small world," said Vivion. "I'm up here to promote, I mean, to find a distributor who'd sell my product. You must know that these days we have, we grow the hottest, most distinctive peppers in the world. I mean we in Trinidad."

"That's what I look at on your shirt. You grow the Moruga Scorpion Red, no?"

"Well, yes. I grow several Reds. But what I'm trying to do is produce some sweeter Moruga Scorpion chilies. Not as hot. You know they got the highest rating last year. Two million Scoville Heat Units."

"Yes, yes. I know is so. Is why I travel. I want to get seeds, maybe hybrid seeds. My farm is new to Kumamoto City. A new agricultural venture for my family. We hope to succeed because of groundwater from volcano, Mt. Aso, makes our soil is rich and fertile."

"You want to propagate Reds in Japan?"

"Yes. I want to make hybrid with Reds, with Scorpions, and others. You see?"

"Of course. You and me and every other professional planter want to make a gentler tastier hybrid. Yes, man! Who serious wouldn't?"

"You try to make hybrid?"

"Well, I have a li'l thing going on the side. You know," evaded Vivion. "Just playing around. No big deal."

Hideo Arata's eager eyes looked to the ground, away from Vivion's face, as he asked, "You have them a lot in Trinidad? The Moruga Reds? Yes?"

Vivion, all at once under pressure to be straightforward, said, "Sure we have them. But you can get them in Jamaica, Antigua, and Barbados, too. In fact, they have several different varieties of Reds over there. All very popular as Bajans partial to they heat."

"Bajans—?"

"Barbados people. We call them Bajans."

Hideo Arata clasped his hands together, then rubbed them right in left, left in right, sharing equally his delight and satisfaction.

As the rattling train rushed smoothly along its tracks.

Viv glanced up at the carriage's LED display showing train stops; he had but two more to go. "Listen man," he said to Hideo Arata, "I getting off next two stops, but I'd really like to talk with you. You mind giving me your number? I could call you sometime this week."

"Yes, yes. Very good. Here's my card with number. I really want more talk about peppers. Maybe we meet tomorrow? What you say?"

Caution instinct hissing alarm, Vivion hesitated as he slid the card into his shirt pocket. Meet tomorrow? That soon? He put his right forefinger between his teeth and gently gnawed. Was this fellow mamaguying him? Was he really that eager, or just some kind of Japanese con-man? But on the other hand, no one could have arranged their being on the same train, in the same carriage, opposite to each other. And then the fellow's open interest in peppers. All of that *had* to be coincidence. Naturally encouraged by the fellow's open interest, Vivion could see a flickering possibility of benefit; a windfall which consequences would perfectly solve his every problem.

Still, and despite Vivion's bone-deep belief that Lady Luck *did* favor him as compensation for being fatherless, it seemed that this casual subway encounter was turning out too right, too sweet, too fast!

Yet the fellow, Hideo Arata, seemed genuine enough. He gave off no aura of deceit and Vivion prided himself on sensing that sort of vibe. This situation seemed to be genuine serendipity; and no one can plan for that. So Vivion made show of shaking his head as if done with a difficult decision and said, "Nah! I just can't, man. Things I have to do. But what about we meet Monday?"

"Good! Good!" said Hideo Arata, beaming agreeably. "You wish meeting at my hotel or your hotel? Yes?"

Vivion thought of his tiny room at the hostel with its cold water sink, the bathroom outside in the common hallway, and decided right away. "I think your place is better," he said. "Mine next to the subway and it kinda noisy."

"Not a problem," said Hideo Arata, "eleven in the morning okay?"

"Perfect, man," said Vivion, as the train decelerated to his stop. "It's great meeting you."

"I see you Monday at eleven then," said Hideo Arata as he stuck out his hand to shake, "Have a good day!"

The door slid open. Vivion released the proffered hand, saying, "You too, mih man." And he was out the carriage.

Spoon's block was comfortable, long-established middle-class. It boasted nice uniform three-story brownstones with blanket-size lawns in front and probably twice that in the back. Some with half-drawn shades, some bare as air, sparkling windows looked out as if curious about the stranger walking by. Solid oak trees, tall and shady, gave the street that special quiet of breeze caressing leaves to shine them. The house numbers were printed black and neat on aluminum mail-boxes with red handles—had Vivion wondering how much the contractor made on that deal. The numbers increasing by two, he estimated that he'd be at Spoon's middle of the next block. And he was just about right; Seven-Seventy-Two was the fourth brownstone on the block.

He'd barely dropped his hand from ringing the bell when the door was flung open. An expression of surprise, then a big smile splitting his face, Spoon grabbed Vivion's hand and pulled him into a sort of vestibule. "Reds!" he laughed out, "Man, what you doing here? Long time no see! I thought it was the mailman. You is the last person I expecting when I open. Man, look at you! You playing Redbeard the pirate with them whiskers? Man, you ent change at all. Look at you in truth. Still skinny as a ram goat. What you living on? Boil grass?" He punctuated every statement with a hearty laugh.

"Spoon, I ent skinny," Vivion protested, "that's just good health and happiness you looking at. Remember, dry bone ent sickness!"

Not so much for wit as occasion, they laughed with each other.

"Come on inside, man," said Spoon and opened a door into a large living room with many pictures and paintings and do-dads on its walls. "Jeanette!" he shouted, "Sweetheart, come and see the scamp I does be telling you about."

From another room came a fine-figured Asian woman in blue jeans cut off at the knees, and an over-size T-shirt that only accented the body beneath. When Vivion's eyes got to her face he met a mischievous smile. She stuck out her hand, said, "That man's been bending my ears going on and on about you. Half the time I think he's telling me about himself, using your name as camouflage."

"It depends on the story he telling. Anything to do with romance, count me out. That's he skill set."

Jeanette laughed. "I thought so! He was never fooling me!"

Spoon broke in, "Me? Fool you? I'd be stoopid to even try. You have Confucius blood in you. All I have is Anancy." He hugged his wife, bussed her on the cheek.

Jeanette shrugged herself out of Spoon's embrace. "Don't hear a word he's saying. But Reds, I'm really glad meeting you. My house is yours." She reached up and kissed his cheek.

Poise lost for a moment at all the given kisses, Vivion said lamely, "Same here, ma'am. Whenever Spoon bring you down, all-you staying by me!"

"So how you prefer me to call you? Reds, or Viv, or Vivion?"

Before he could answer, Spoon interjected, "Call him Mr. Vivion. You didn't hear him call you 'Ma'am' just now?

"Harry!" said Jeanette, joking but serious. "Give the boy a break! Anyhow, I'll call you Viv. I like it. It's short and to the point. I'll leave 'Reds' between you two old-timers."

"Old-timers!" was the fellas outraged chorus.

Jeanette, snickering, said, "Now I have to cook," and went away.

Grown up in a bungalow with rooms that had side doors—at least two each—which led to adjacent rooms, for Vivion this room-after-room, train carriage-style house was very different. Still, Spoon seemed to have adjusted. Here in the first of this opened-ended space he was clearly at peace. Set against the side wall, he had installed an elaborate music system. Shooting bragging eyes at Vivion, he punched quiet green LED buttons that turned on a set of Old Timers calypsoes.

He asked, "Still Old Oak?" and while he made drinks the Mighty Terror came on, sympathizing with and advising against Santa Claus living a lonely life since he had no wife.

"Yuh crib nice, man," said Vivion.

"You don't have to tell me," said Spoon as he handed a tall glass halved with rum to Vivion. "So how you get the address?"

"Mervyn Charles. Bounce up with him in Macy's . . . "

"Mervyn! Same old Merv, eh. That man is a living data bank. He know everybody business."

"I'll drink to that," said Vivion. And that they did. More than once.

Spoon had not changed much. Same remarkable skin with its pampered look, hairless and smooth as glass. A little added weight around the neck and belly. But still happy as a lark, laughing at every recollection of their escapades. Then, prompted by nostalgia, Spoon put on another CD of old-time calypsoes which soon had both of them humming along as they sipped superior Old Oak. Jeanette, cracking wise about this and that with every trip, was in and out the living room bearing ginger-flavored teas and hot, delicious dim sum finger foods.

As the boys back then would say, "A great lime was had by all!"

When the conversation drifted to how each was spending their days, Spoon, eyes all at once glistening, went off about being a father, "Boy! You wouldn't believe it. I mean the joy you does get. I mean, I wouldn't have believed it. Lemme tell you straight. The first time was from Conrad, the first boy, two years old, a baby hardly could talk. The first time he say 'I love Da-Da' plain as ever, I wept. Like I doing now."

He paused, grinning wide as he swabbed his eyes then blew his nose in his front shirt tails. And still sporting the silly grin, went on. "I don't know about you. You had a better life. Always had connections. Listen, man. I know you since you was a kid, when we was kids. You did whatever you wanted and there was no problem. You probably always heard 'I love you.' But brother, not so yuh boy here. I never hear dat purest 'I love you' until mih own children tell me. You hearing me, man? I never knew how much or what I had missed until then. And that missing part of me is what does still cry."

Vivion listened, sympathetic, feeling so exactly of what Spoon was saying. Knowing it probably more profoundly because of his one-party origins. Still, the passion of the outburst surprised him. Spoon was of nice respectable family; two girls, then third try lucky, a boy who so relieved Mr. Douglas that he named his son Junior as his first name with the middle name being Harold, which was also the father's first. This behavior made sense only because of an old folks saying that 'it takes a man to make a boy.'

Although there is another that preaches 'it takes a real man to make a female.'

So who knows what.

The puzzle that occupied Vivion's thoughts was 'What could've been so terrible in a family, a regular storybook household like Spoon's? The Harold Douglas house . . .'

Mid-thought, Jeanette bounced in to serve up them a new batch of dim sum taste treats seasoned with her off-beat humor—"How long did Cain hate Abel? Answer: As long he was able!"—which changed the 'painful past' part of the mood. So then, she sitting on his lap, Spoon moved on to how and when he and Jeanette first met, "It was after, what? Maybe two dates, we still real formal with Miss Lui, Mr. Douglas, while in my mind is time to stop that foolishness. So I tell her that in my culture, we Trini culture, a courting couple does have 'sweet' names for each other. Sometimes is even ordinary 'Darling.' So she all for dat. Yes, man, we was really in love. The real thing, I mean. So she decide she like 'Sweetheart.' Is a picture and a taste in one, she say. So dat's my sweet-name for she. So I tell her my nickname is 'Spoon' and she look at me saying, "That's it? Geng!" Is only months later after we fix up and everything, that she explain. Is because they got a lotsa people name Geng in China where her parents come from. So the name itself had no romance value. Although now she say she did get to like it . . . "

Vivion let him talk away, enjoying the music, the nostalgia, the sound of Spoon's voice, accent becoming more and more Trinidadian the longer he spoke. His wife gone, the tales had moved on to how he and Jeanette had created a taxi service business that he managed from home with four black important-looking full-sized sedans, and how the deal was extra sweet because the cars were really 'third hand acting like second hand' and he had paid only a tenth of their real value because the salesman was heavy into drugs and . . .

Vivion lost contact with the story. In a funk for no exact reason, a notion had crept out of his subconscious that he was kinda tired of tales of Spoon's brilliance and successes. First was his beautiful wife, then it was his loveable children. Vivion also had a beautiful lady, a fine 'wife' in every way. A gorgeous woman who, in his presence, a limer had once declared, "Miss Lovely Lady! You sweeter than curry bhagii with cilantro and nutmeg flavors!" Then he looked at Vivion and nodded respect to him.

Though he couldn't exactly pull the pot together, Vivion understood that the described taste was intended as an extreme compliment.

But when Spoon had shifted to his prospering business, it rankled that he went on like there was some special genius to riding Opportunity, or buying low to sell high. And back of his mind Vivion couldn't help feeling that any special business savvy at all came from the Jeanette's side of this equation.

So when Spoon now paused to freshen their glasses, by an impulse he couldn't deny, Vivion raised his voice a casual just-so-much and said, "Funny, eh. Everybody doing they own thing. Making waves. Like how I have this li'l pepper farm venture now going on the third year."

It got Spoon's attention. He stopped mid-pouring, turned a puzzled face to Vivion, and said, "Pepper farm! You mean peppers?"

"Yep. Hot peppers too. I mean, I growing, farming five acres of peppers. Hot Moruga Scorpion red peppers and others. You know, Seven Pot, Three Pot, Habañero, Scotch Bonnet, and so on. You know."

Spoon looked at Vivion, made ineffectual motions with his hands as he said, "Reds, what you know about peppers? From Moruga or otherwise?"

Vivion, buoyed again and happy to give his friends a précis of the hot peppers business looked around for Jeanette. But she was gone. So he poured it all on Spoon. He mentioned the Scoville Scale, and that Moruga Scorpion Red had beat two million units. Just as he used to do when they limed on their bench, he showed off his knowledge in the exotic field.

He counted off on his fingers, the dozen varieties he worked with on his farm these days. "I have pure-line Scotch Bonnet, and Habañero, and hybrid Big Sun. All three got tolerable heat. Then I have Tiger Teeth, one of two varieties, from Barbados. The other is Wirri-Wirri which is hotter. I mean they could actually scorch yuh tongue. Then from little nook-and-cranny gardens all over Trinidad and Tobago, I have Faria, green and yellow types, Hooded Peter peppers, Congo pepper, Seven Pot, Moruga red, and Moruga yellow. These are among the hottest peppers in the world. As I said, two million units hot on Scoville. Think a' that. I mean dat is hot enough to make you cry, to scald yuh tongue, then yuh guts, and then yuh arsehole. I mean, they so hot they's got to be Satan favorite."

Aware he was prattling, but squeezing reassurance from Spoon's seeming interest, he explained, " Is why I up here, man. I looking for a distributor. Nothing positive yet, but I still have some meetings to go—"

Perhaps to change the topic, Spoon jumped in, "—you meaning like job interviews?" and both hid relief in roars of agreeable laughter that left the peppers patter hanging there. Then they clinked glasses in toasts to the marvel of Life's unexpected outcomes.

Time flying, it was just after five o'clock when, promising to try to squeeze in another hang-out during the coming week, they broke it up. Spoon and Jeanette trapped him in the little vestibule to the outside door and gave him the parting kisses and hugs routine. Vivion suffered through it with a good face and felt oddly free as he closed the street gate. His only regret was never seeing Spoon's kids. They were spending the day with cousins, Jeanette's brother's kids, in Queens. Children who, judging from their parents good looks, Vivion could only imagine how beautiful they'd be.

On thinking of them he could neither explain or identify the subtle tightening in his guts.

Trussed up Land Crabs

ooOoo

NIKKI WAS PAINTING, ANDALUZA reflective, sitting in her rocker quieter than usual.

"So what you think about the farm?" asked Andaluza.

"Farm? What farm?"

"You know, the pepper farm. Vivion and he peppers."

"O! You mean the garden! That grand experiment. Another of his ingenious ideas. That's all it is. You know, like the house, self-sufficient and everything," said Nikki in amused, indulgent tones as she work her fan brush delicately on the canvas.

Andaluza studied her for a long moment before restarting her rocker to a thoughtful rhythm. Time passed.

Nikki broke the quiet, "I thought you was behind that whole thing."

"Yes," agreed Andaluza, nodding absently. "I still behind it."

"Well, for one thing it does keep him busy. Occupy he

restless mind, if you know what I mean."

"So you don't have nothing to do with it?"

"Me? No Andaluza. What I know about peppers, about gardening in general, is like smoke in a thimble. No, not me, darling. I is a working artist. My window view is the bubbly creek with flowery banks and high woods in the background. That is my artist view. Peaceful as paint waiting for use. Waiting for life. Hoping that it'll please."

"So you does never check on the farm, the garden? On how it going or thing like that?"

"What use that going to be, Andaluza? First, I have to go to the other side of the house to see that. But more than that, the whole garden scene is boring. It so orderly, look at it and you thinking sweat and hard labor. Not for me, darling. I telling you next painting I make is a sign saying 'Artist at Work' and I putting it up over mih door. Lemme tell you something. Being an artist ent easy. I didn't realize at first, but talent does change you inside out. You from the same race and place as others but talent make you altogether different. Is about how you see the world and how the world see you. Is about teaching yuh self what you value most. For me as a woman, and I mean as a Black woman, Serena and Halle Berry and J Lo make me proud to love and value me, mih-self, and I. Yes! Them round-bottom women show me that every shade in Black is beautiful. Is same thing when it come to music. I love Lata Mangeshkar and Ruby Khan and Asha Bhosle with they sweet, high, impossible voices sounding like Kathleen Battle gone exotic. Same way I feel for Miriam Makeba in she passion, Shakira with she rhythmic hips, and we own Calypso Rose with she sweaty energy—"

Andaluza had put her hand up, saying softly, "Not cutting you, but Makeba is mih favorite singer. Forbidden Games is still the song in mih heart. With that song Miriam put truest feelings into sweet melody."

Moved by her wistful tone, Nikki said, "Guess that's what the Americans call soul, eh. For me, mih spirit satisfy with the little talent and the lots a' pleasure that it have. And I telling you straight. My major pleasure is watching women, women like you, and me, make it."

Head cocked sideways, contemplative, Andaluza looked at Nikki long, then chuckled and said, "Child, you's a funny one! A bit off in yuh head, but you all right."

A blush blooming at her neck from the compliment, Nikki tried a comeback, "You is the funny one," the weak retort only enhancing the burn.

Fried Bakes

ooOoo

MENTION OF HIS PEPPER BUSINESS to Spoon had brought
Hideo Arata back to mind, and Vivion was almost locked
into his salesman persona by the time he got to the hostel.
At once to his backpack, he took out his notebook—some
twenty pages all about growing peppers professionally.
Notes assembled from thorough research, and categorized
into ideas and recommendations. His important topics
varied: from planning production and choosing varieties to
field and soil preparation; from fertility management to crop
care and diseases; from seedling production to harvest
operations. Last on his list was financial analyses, there only
because he realized that potential business partners would
consider it significant.

Vivion's working theory was that personal charm
backed up by mastery of such solid data was an unbeatable
strategy for winning over partners. So he used his notes to
review matters which these businessmen, these managers
would likely ask. He read up on which peppers were in

greatest demand. Where were the best sources for seeds of most popular varieties. How to determine the purchasing power of farmers, which was in turn suggested by the way they regulated plantings and pickings to suit the best months for business. He read his notes on the best methods of produce grading and packaging; on the preferred placement and construction of seedling nurseries; and although he did not believe in them, even the most dependable Plant Growth Regulators available.

He had maverick ideas on the subject of PGRs. Although agreeing that sterilants and insecticides could be necessary, he preferred and had always tried for a natural way to keep his farm close to ecological neutrality. A chemical footprint of a minus factor. So for nitrogen feeding, he planted pigeon peas and red beans between his pepper plants. Here and there, he planted lemon grass and wild flowers whose nectar enticed ants which encouraged small lizards, and various birds, and even grasshoppers that control pests like aphids and leaf cutters. Of most crucial importance, he set up two hives which in the years had quadrupled in size and honey production and ensured prompt pollination of his pepper plants.

Pacing the small room, Vivion read and rehearsed until near midnight when he took a lay-down to rest tired eyes that had serviced a contented mind. He reassured himself that on Monday morning when he met Hideo Arata from Japan, he would be impressive. He'd be casual and self-deprecating. He'd be informative as a search engine. So if Mister Hideo was at all serious about creating hybrids of Moruga Red Scorpions, he'd most likely bite, and become just the sort of business partner Vivion wished for; one Far-East away from Trinidad who was wealthy, ambitious, and hopefully, willing to pay a good price for premium hot peppers.

As he stretched a wide yawn that counseled sleep, he kept his focus on making this windfall happen. This Japanese fella was no fool. That his family entrusted him with their restaurant business said a lot. So Vivion had to be up for a superior challenge. Bring out his A game. Be subtle yet straightforward. Lighthearted though serious. Informative without being boring. In a word, the pitchman perfect. Because this prize at stake was more than profit, dignity, or self-confidence. For should this play go his way, success at getting a Japanese pepper contract would well prove to himself his own maturity and competence.

And athletics, education, and earlier, easy accomplishments aside, at last he'd have achieved something that was really challenging!

Lying down, half asleep and feeling good, his mind wandered restless here and there, present and past, until it got around to his Nikki and settled down and spun him a golden memory.

He had gone to an art show with his regular crew—one of them had received the invite—and had reached that point when he decided to slip off and be away. It had been a nice party so far; nice people dressed smartly making clever statements about this and that, Vivion himself being a major perpetrator.

Still as usual, bottom line, he was bored to the marrow

in his bones. So, well into his disappearing routine, he had already wandered into various rooms and areas, gradually distancing himself from the crew. He was now eyeing a hallway that led to the house's front door, his Exit destination. In between, there was one open door from which came the buzz of cheery party chatter.

Vivion decided. Three long steps and he'd swift past it and be out through the front door in a blink.

Just then through the buzzing doorway came two women—although only one was really there and mattered. She was tall and shapely, her skin the color of dusk lightened by sunset's glow. Her face was a happy place, vibrant, on the brink of a smile. Maybe what she was thinking, her eyes twinkled with delight, looking everywhere, seeking for fun. She wore a brief pale blue thing that bared her shoulders and navel, in which there sparkled a gem. The pants were a navy blue skin-tight hip-hugging tissue with white lace trim at the ankles. Her open-toed sandals were golden, her toenails silvered. She was a beautiful genie fresh out the bottle, and her bouquet as she walked past him was a splendid confusion with hints of nutmeg and coriander and orange blossoms.

In a word, absolutely, stunningly, marvelous!

As their eyes made four, Vivion gushed, "Forgive me, Miss Angel, but would you care to be part of my enduring heart program?"

Her eyes narrowed for a moment and the space between them sprouted tiny puckers which were swiftly gone as puzzlement departed and her face was again just lovely. She went on her way without a word.

Then Vivion lost his poise when, with a lazy graceful twist of torso, she cast back at him an amused, superior look. All at once trite and foolish, his clever comebacks turned tail and deserted. Still, compelled to respond, make some sort of approach, he pushed his way through people to catch up with her. Then from off to the left, near the bar, a voice called out, "Shani! Shani!" and she turned, looked that way and started towards a smiling Indian fellow in a black business suit that seemed out of place.

Yet Mr. Business Suit was a better-favored man than Vivion; he knew this daydream on a first name basis.

Vivion watched as they bussed each other on both cheeks European style, waited a half a minute more as they exchanged whatevers, then he approached, stuck his hand out and said to the fellow, "Hi, man. I'm Vivion. Sorry to interrupt, but you are?"

"Oh, hello. I'm Sinannan Singh."

"Have to say that's a great name. Has a lot of, of what is it?" he turned to Shani and winked, "assonance? Or is it consonance? Can you help? Please?"

"Well, sir, seeing it's you, it'd most probably be *ass*onance. Don't you think? What you say Singh?"

Singh wasn't into it at all. With a high deflective shrug, he said, "Look, man, I'm a civil engineer. I barely could talk English."

That she had called him by the neutral 'Singh' irrationally pleased Vivion. He stuck his hand out to Shani and said, "Well, I'm still Vivion and I'm just north of thrilled to meet you."

"Me, too. Charmed I'm sure, Mr. Vivion. I'm Shanika

Grant-Ali."

"Well, that explains it."

"Explains what?" asked Shanika.

"Your name. Shani. You're of North-Arabian descent. One of those visiting . . . how you call them? Sprites? Spirits? Djinni? Genies? Yes, that's it! Rhymes with Shani, eh. They tend to have magical qualities similar to yours. Not earthbound. But that aside, what you should know is that you've made your Vivion here, a very happy fella. I have actually met and greeted a dream that I have dreamt for a long time. So I'll now go sit in the gallery and reflect on my exceptional fortune." He took her hand, bowed and kissed it, then turned to Singh and clapped him on the shoulder, saying, "Relish your moment of star shine, my man, Singh. You will sleep well tonight!"

Then off he went to the gallery and sat hoping for the best.

And after interminable minutes, she came and sat and talked with him.

That's how they began.

ooOoo

JUST AFTER MIDDAY, MINUTES after Nikki arrived at the bungalow, a cool wet breeze began easing down through the backyard conifers. Tone peevish, Andaluza said, "Child, like you bring a coolness jumbie with you, or what! How it gone cold so?"

Only that "Child" was first out her mouth stopped Nikki from taking the older woman to task. She said instead, "Andaluza, it not that cold. Forecast say is drizzling rain all evening and going on throughout the night." She used the exact words of the morning's weatherman and tried for his vocal delivery.

Imitation good enough for Andaluza to snigger and say, "Them radio people have no idea. They just guessing. We may as well look up in the sky and check how the clouds blowing."

Practical as ever, Nikki said, "So why you don't throw on a sweater or something. Keep in yuh body heat while we make some hot chocolate."

Andaluza shrugged and grimaced, "I have a better idea. I'll put on the sweater and we'll go lime in the cellar."

"Cellar? All-you have a cellar?"

"You forgetting this was mih father's house. Listen child, every colonial aristocrat had a cellar. He had to have it for letting fruit liquors mature and that could take two, two and a half, even three years. He'd use it for priming wine and rum and jellies and that sorta things. A cool dark place is essential for that. It might sound funny, but you have to remember they was still Europeans representing their homeland cultures. How to make alcohol. What do with fruits to pass through winter. They couldn't believe in they luck down here. They was always preparing for winter worst."

Nikki listened past a tinge of defensiveness as she definitely understood. It was different with the Europeans, but so many times she had had to stand up for her own mixed race and culture parentage. "So let we go, nuh," she said.

Andaluza started off into the house saying, "But first lemme get something to amuse we mouth, eh."

The cellar was a cool quiet solid room that shortened as you went further in—seven feet as you entered and dropping to a two-foot crawl space hacked out of the earth at the very last of the fifteen or so feet. Except for the door, the walls all around were halved logs placed cut faces overlapping in and out against each other, the intervening seams plastered over with white clay tapia. The vertical lines of alternating color, one strong dark brown, the other fragile and pale, suggested protection. Insects, hot air, loud noises, whatever might be, no threat to peace and quiet could get into this cave.

Nikki liked it right away.

They settled down, Nikki in a deep comfortable leather chair, Andaluza in yet another rocking chair. Refreshments on the serving tray were guava jelly on crackers, ripe papaya in bite-size chunks, two mango Johns, and a thermos of cold coconut water. Taste wise, the selection was judged 'Excellent' by consensus as they partook of the treats.

Sipping with her eyes closed as she rocked slowly, Andaluza asked, "So how the two a' you meet?

"I was wondering when you would ask," said Nikki. "But what you should better ask is when I first see him."

"Well, what else you think I asking?"

"Hold yuh horses, Andaluza. Don't you go short and sharp with me. If you patient I going tell you everything."

Andaluza turned her head and looked off at the crawlspace.

Nikki sniffed noisily and switched off laser beams she had flashed at the older woman. She sipped of her fresh coconut water, and continued in a slower, patient voice, "You see, as it was, I had heard Vivion speaking at an art showing before I met him. Okay! Lemme back up some more. I know, I know. You be patient. About a year after mih family come back home from New York, mih best friend Rita Chapin get selected by some big-time art people to be part of a 'Promising Talents' show. They say she was one of the designated masters-to-be. She work get a whole wall to itself. The complete, entire wall! That's how much the judges thought of Rita!

"Notwithstanding all a' that, her chubby boyfriend, Mr. Oswin Payne, a fella who struggled part-time at making whispery so-so pencil portraits, fell into a jealous sulk. So expected! Said he wouldn't go with her to the presentation. Said he'd be busy. The wuss!

"This Oswin is a privileged son born halfway between four older and younger sisters. Pride and joy of he parents, most likely because of tepid promise as a junior government funds manager, in those days he was becoming a popular choice in the marrying meets. So, Love also being Stupid, Rita submit to his bullshit and decide she wouldn't do the gig either. 'My Oswin is more important than some outdated old men's praises,' she fool she self to say.

"Outdated old men's praises! From she mouth to my ears, those were his words about the people in this land who could make a painter's name and fame.

"So in the security of mih room I went to work and two hours of hard words it took for me to convince Rita different—that she must attend and smile and say 'Thank you' a lot, and patiently describe she stuff to whoever was curious.

"So we went. And not saying it was all because of me, but everything turn out wonderful for Rita. Best of all she drop Oswin. All that jealous sulking was only making 'im fatter."

"That's jealousy for you," pronounced Andaluza with a heavy sigh, "Child, lemme tell you something. Jealousy will kill you. One way or the other it is poison to yuh body and soul and it certainly will kill you."

Nikki put up a defensive hand. "Don't put me in that

ward, Mammy. That ent me at all. How I see it, nobody does own anybody else. Is slavery if that going down. As far as I see, when it come to stuff like sentiments and passions and such matters of the heart, people should only do as they really feel," she paused to catch and hold Andaluza's eyes. "Is how I feel about Vivion, I mean, er, yuh boy, yuh son. From the first talk we talk, I know I'll always love that boy and the man inside him. And I is a one man, one love woman." Though feeling not at all shy, she was blushing deeply as she finished.

"You better drink some coconut water," suggested a smiling Andaluza. "Cool down that passion and then tell me how you meet 'im."

"Oh yes, back to that. But wait! Can I just call you Anda? Please! Not that Andaluza is too long, or anything. Is just that I does take so long to tell a story anyhow and I don't want to lose any extra time saying yuh—"

"Well," cut in Andaluza, "I never hear such a crock a' what breed maggots? Ain't you the boldest? Okay. Call me Anda for today. Just get on with the damn story before night jumbie come ketch we."

"Thank you so very much," said Nikki in a snooty voice. Then she switched to a coquette's tease, "You don't frighten me at all, Missus Andaluza. You just playing bad because you know I like you. So, as I was saying, I heard Vivion talking before actually meeting him. This is how it happen. Sunday of the previous week, I had shown three pieces at another girlfriend, Janice Peters', gallery. Insurance claims adjuster by day, she managed this after-hours art gallery Friday to Sunday evenings, from nine-ish to around midnight. Financial worth-the-while came from the unlicensed liquor bar that she husband, Rupert, served to wash down his cook-ups. And Rupert's cook-ups really special. Like pigeon peas and rice to go with dasheen-leaf callaloo. Or peppery bake-and-shark with rum-and-coconut water as coolant. Some nights it could be corn bread with saltfish buljohl, or curried blue crabs, and so forth. Everything delicious. Every dish a favorite. With Rupert you accept whatever he hand you, for although erratic, he was a truly outstanding cook. Among the artsy-fartsy circles, his menu had become the latest must.

"So there's yuh girl playing rabbit with a celery stick, chatting with Janice while flirting with she Grenadian cousin, Kenyon Andrews, since it seemed that on mih first entry into the living room, I mean while I was still saying "Hellos" to people, he telling Janice that he fall for, and chose me as the One. He wasn't shy about letting me know about it either. Said how all his born days he had been waiting for One such as I. Said my appeal wasn't just pure beauty. Though that counted fine, there was also the bounce in mih step, and the way mih smiles does light up a room, and there was, too, mih amazing warmth of manner.

"I mean he coulda been casting yuh girl for Miss Universe. Made me feel great. He was well-spoken, amusing, and self-confident, details I admire in a man. And he kept saying the right things most girls want to hear. Little did he know *my* truth that I am *so* immune to flattery about mih looks. I knew right away that Kenyon and I could never be. My basic feeling is that I had nothing to do with how I look. I just born that way! For me, in spite of mih bright smiley responses, any thrill of a "You're-so-beautiful" approach is dulled by its staleness. Can't help it. Always felt that way.

"After a while, I supposing for hostess reasons Janice slipped away, leaving us on we own. So curious about his opinion, I gradually steered Kenyon closer to mih paintings. Artist's vanity? What I could say! The pieces were hung in a tight triangle. I had objected to that, saying it was too cramped, but the experts prevail. The pieces were my concept of local paranormals; a snarling La Diablesse with dripping fangs from a bloody she-devil mouth; two yellow-eyed Douens with their prominent oversize back-to-front feet; and a bat-faced Soucouyaun preparing to shed she skin into a mortar.

"You have to understand. I try to make mih work accessible. Nobody have to be a connoisseur or expert to get my stuff. Some learned folks use categories like native and primitive to describe mih paintings. They don't know what they talking about. I think that any true art, especially *my* art, is a direct communication with the viewer's soul. If they feel it, they got it. It does appeal without explanation. It might be of night-time terrors, or contrary images that make we shiver. Great art of any sort does put us in touch with imagined destinies. It does bare we self to hidden guilts, to covered up misdeeds, to wished-for but undeserved glories. To all kinda things, bad and good.

"Good Art does make something physical out a' fears and hopes and dreams. So all art, no matter what, is relevant and mostly beyond categorizing.

"And that's why I put up them paintings."

Andaluza raised her hand like a school child with a

question. "You really feeling that strong about it, eh! How long you making paintings?"

"Ever since I small, seven, eight, in elementary school, I like drawing things," said Nikki. "You know, regular things like a hand, or a mango, or how a hat does rest on a head. Li'l things like that. But they weren't paintings. I only learn about painting in school in New York. Mr. Jay Hinkson, the ninth grade art teacher, sort of discovered mih talent. Is he that introduce me to the passion, the do-it-right detail, the discipline parts of it."

Andaluza nodded at the answer and both women sipped their drinks in the quiet cave-like cellar. Then Nikki returned her glass to the tray and continued, "Well when I get Kenyon to my triad, standing before them making comments was a little group—three vague shades of attractive young women, an amused mature fella who was laughing a lot, and an attentive teenager who could have been the mature man's son—all of them being entertained by a tall, fair-skinned, broad-shouldered young fella with baby dreads under a floppy cricket hat, and a distinctive voice.

"Kind of seductive baritone and husky at the same time. A playful, taunting voice. I ent shame to say that right away something in he raspy tones thrill mih stomach and rev up mih imagination. And his manner was something else again. Clearly bogus! Because despite all the highfaluting comments, you get the idea that he was just being clever. Acting a smart-ass to amuse the group. Being witty maybe to own the center of attention.

"I couldn't wait for 'im to turn my way so I could see he

face.

"Just then the group burst out in guffaws at some especially keen sally. Which was all right as far as it goes. Except it seemed that the funny comment was about *my* work. So more than anything I wanted to know, to get an idea of, what he had said.

"Didn't get opportunity to act, though. For that's when, maybe mih distracted manner, when Mr. Kenyon Andrews went macho on yuh girl. Grabbed mih shoulders and nodding vigorous at yours truly, announced, 'Shanika, try to follow me. Please!'

"Well! I scarcely hear the words for he rudeness. Putting hands on me! What he thinking? He out he mind? I stare 'im down as I shrug mih-self out he grip and turn to get away from making the scene a horror show.

"But he dance in front me, saying, 'Listen Shanika. Listen, girl. I'm so, so really sorry. Don't know what . . . '

"Well I stab mih finger at he face space and hiss out like a alley cat, 'Mister, you get out of mih way. Right now! Or take a slap like a fool right here in the middle a' the room!'

"Only then, looking pathetic, he get out a' mih way.

"So I went out on the terrace to cool off and was there five minutes or so when I see Mr. Intriguing Baby-Dreads entertainer run down the front stairs and set off for the main road all by himself alone.

"But that solitary departure cheer me up right away.

"Then Tuesday morning, on the phone about what we did or didn't do over the weekend, I mentioned the whole episode to Rita Chapin and it stirred up a memory for her. 'Was he sort of light-skinned, with reddish curly hair?'

"'Could be. He had on a hat. I only really saw the back of he neck. The baby dreads looked kinda soft, though.'

"'Tall, eh!'

"'Yeah! Tall but not too tall. Maybe six three, six four.'

"'Well, you six foot yourself—'

"Okay, Andaluza, lemme tell you this straight off. I sensitive about mih height, okay. As a girl growing up, I was always too tall. Tallest in class. The one they asking to pick the high fruit. So I don't welcome height comments. And Rita well know this. So right off I correct she. 'Rita Chapin,' I tell she, 'I is five eleven. Not six feet. Five eleven, okay!'

"But she don't pay me no mind. Just keep on talking. Shut me down. 'Nikki,' she say, 'one inch don't make a difference one way or the other. You just tall for a woman!'

"But needing she help, I swallow spit and give up, moved on. 'Rita, I don't know who he is. Except that he voice was unusual, kinda husky and nice. If you know what I mean . . . ?' I trail off weak, feeling a little foolish.

"Then with she kinda superior chuckle, Rita Chapin ups with, 'Listen darling, I might have a idea who you talking about. That raspy voice is the clue. I'll do a check around.'

"I said, 'Rita, you're the best,' and really meant it.

"So long story short, that's how, the following weekend, Vivion Pinheiro get invited to Rita's party."

Forehead furrowed, Andaluza gave Nikki a look sharp with puzzlement and dissatisfaction. "What you mean 'long story short'? Tell me the 'how'!"

"Well okay, okay, Missus! Calm yuh self. Once she remembered, Rita arrange everything. You see when she was in UWI couple years before, she went to this competition that a tall light-skinned fella win. It was an open competition—meaning open to everybody, professional or amateur—and after everything was said and done, the judges unanimously awarded Red-skinned first prize. Curious about the homey, Rita went to the library trying to find the poem he read. But no luck, although the librarian had heard of it. 'It's a strong poem,' she opined, 'but they say it's his speaking it, his voice is what made the whole thing coalesce. Gave it feeling. At least, that's what is said!'

"Rita stuck with the search and eventually found out the fella's name. Then as time pass, of course she forget it. Although the special-voice remain in she mind. So when I mention *my* similar impression, it trigger a bell, and being Miss Knowledgeable about odds and favorites in the local bachelors' sweepstakes, she knew exactly how to locate the man behind the hoarse vocals.

"Which is what she did and invited yuh Vivion. Then in the party we kinda meet up and hit it off. I like how he was boyish and willing to laugh and take things easy. Like me. Right away I knew that if we get together, because of them strengths, I'd forgive he weaknesses. It didn't take long to know we was certain about each other, like on the same page, and well, as you know, I move in with 'im. And we happy as ever. So that's really the end of story, except for, with the warmest hugs, here's to Rita Chapin. My man-finder friend!" said she, and raised her glass of cool coconut water.

ooOoo

THE HOSTEL'S ROOM-RADIO CAME on at five thirty a.m. as Vivion had set it to do. The station played light classical music, soothing sounds that eased his transition to daytime and duty. He obeyed bodily demands to the bathroom, then put on sweats and went for his usual jog in the Park.

Back around seven, he showered and had breakfast at the corner bodega. By nine o'clock he was dressed for his date with contract Destiny, as in Hideo Arata, the hot pepper baron from Japan. The off-white polo shirt of Saturday was rumpled from sink-washing and needed ironing, so this time he wore the light blue one. The Pinheiro Peppers logo in flaming red letters looked good on this shirt as well.

Dressed too early and ready to go, Vivion went and stood by the open window and looked at the street. A long black limo stopped at the red light, its right turn indicator clicking time to freedom, then graceful for such a cumbersome machine, turned and with surprising quiet passed beneath him. Long minutes later, nothing else happening out there, he went and fiddled with the radio, trying for something other than his favorite light classics. All he could get was static. So around nine-twenty-eight, restless as a tick-tocking second hand, he gave up on the cramping space and went downstairs.

Rawlston John was behind the counter listening to an all news radio station. He looked up and with a hearty laugh as if the greeting was funny, asked, "So how Trini-man making out?"

"Everything is everything!" said Vivion.

"Yeah, dat's de trick, man. Take she as she goes," agreed Rawlston John. Then in a lower excited gossipy tone, he continued, "You hear wha' dey saying 'bout Usain? Dat is de yam he eating make 'im so fast?"

Vivion had read of the report by some Olympic body, but relishing the empty talk, he exclaimed, "You making joke, man. Really?"

And just as he wished, they wasted some gratifying minutes chatting about Olympic and international outrageousness, bias, and envy.

Vivion broke the lime with Rawlston John around ten when he got the idea to walk to the address on Hideo's card; sixtieth street near Columbus Circle. Maybe a mile or so from the hostel, he'd go south along Central Park West and easily get there in good time.

Walking the pavement lost in aimless thought, at an intersection he looked up at the street sign and saw it was sixty-sixth. He crossed the street and a few steps on saw a couple sitting on a park bench arm-in-arm, laughing with each other. From clothes and manner, retired well off and securely idling through the idyllic age. Vivion approached them and greeted, "Hi folks."

They looked up at him, two pairs of steel-rimmed glasses on pleasant faces that gleamed a wordless "Yes?"

"Well," said Vivion, "you folks seem so happy together I get the feeling you wouldn't mind me asking you the time."

The woman said, "Why, of course not—" she glanced at her wrist, "it's—"

"— time to buy a watch!" interjected the man.

At which the couple succumbed to an attack of titters. Although the woman paused to say, "It's twenty to eleven, dear" and was back giggling with her man by the time Vivion could say, "Thanks."

A soft smile on his face, he started for Columbus Circle.

Vivion double-checked the address on Hideo Arata's business card and confirmed that this building had the same number. He looked again at the business card and noticed that Mr. Arata's room number was 4307, and putting that together with the building being a typical New York skyscraper, realized that Hideo Arata occupied a room on the forty-third floor of this grand hotel. A room approximately six hundred and fifty feet up in the air. Clearly in another climate.

For no actual reason, all that height was bothersome.

Another part of the intimidation was that the building had an enormous lobby visible from the sidewalk through broad merry-go-round glass doors that released the passenger to a pair of purple-suited doormen obviously stationed there to interrogate and make judgments vis-à-vis further entry.

Vivion shot a glance at the doormen and figured they were taking notice of him. He walked out of their line of vision, turned at the street corner and stood next to a fire hydrant worrying his under-lip tender as he pondered the situation.

After coming to a firm decision, he wasted four, five minutes strolling up and down the cross street. Then time up, he went directly to the right side round-about door, entered and was spun through to the waiting doorman.

"Can I help you, sir?" the fellow said politely.

"Yes, you can, sir," said Vivion and proffered Hideo's business card, "I'm supposed to meet a friend here at this time and he ent show up. Can you contact him for me, please. He might be still in he room. Number forty-three zero seven. Here." He gave the card to the doorman.

The doorman briefly studied the card, returned it and pointed, "You should go over to Reception. They'd take care of it."

Vivion said, "Thank you, sir" and worked at a swagger to Reception.

A young woman with large, make-up blackened eyes, and lips painted bright red asked, "How can I help you, sir," and Vivion handed her the card and told his tardy friend tale again.

The woman compared the business card to data on her computer console and declared, "No problem, sir. If you use that house phone, I'll call his number and you can speak to him."

Vivion picked up the indicated phone and heard Hideo saying, "Hallo, yes. Hallo?"

"Hey, Hideo," said Vivion, "is Vivion Pinheiro. The pepper fella." He put a smile into the words.

"Yes, of course. You come right up. Turn left when you get out of the lift. My door is number seven. It is open."

"Hold on, Hideo. That's just it. I don't want to come up. Is such a pleasant day, I suggesting we walk and talk in the Park. Man, it really nice outside. What you say?"

"Not a problem, Vivion Pinheiro. I really prefer walking in the Park. I'll be five minutes."

"Great!" said Vivion, "I waiting in the street."

"Okay then, goodbye for now," said Hideo Arata.

They entered the Park at the Columbus Circle fifty-ninth street entrance and headed East along the walking path. Far from being alone, they saw crouched intent bikers flashing by; smiling joggers in their blissful zones; lovers yielding to urges to hug and kiss; nannies, too restless to sit, pushing open strollers. It seemed that everyone who could was enjoying the exceptional autumn weather.

Vivion observed, "I think this is the City's best season. I mean I've only been here during summers and autumns, and I know I'd hate winter. Would be too, too cold. As a season, Spring to me isn't much more than a potential. Summer is too much like home, minus the variety of fruits. But autumn, autumn is special. All them beautiful landscapes. The cool enough weather. The long, long days of warm sunshine. It's all great, man. Then you go out a' the city itself. Is a bigger-size picture postcard. Colors in the hills. Leaves golden on the ground. Man, it just plain grand."

"At home our autumn is beautiful too. But it is short," said Hideo.

"How so?"

"Well, it is a factor of geography. Our archipelago lies on a Rim of Fire, the source of volcanoes, earthquakes, tsunamis. Then because of that location, the winds bring us typhoons and out-of-season snow storms. We are tested by the weather. We are tested by climate. But most significant, we are tested by the inexorable shiftings of our Earth's mantle. Nature is an unfeeling, violent force to my country. We have to make the best of it."

Impressed by Hideo's oratory, and for no other reason than the thought he shouldn't as he did, Vivion murmured, "We have volcanoes too—"

At which Hideo stopped and turned an astonished face to him. "You have volcanoes?" he exclaimed.

"Yeah! Mud volcanoes. They spout up about one, two feet and shoot out mud bubbles."

"Mud bubbles!" repeated Hideo, his face all at once brightening to a ruddy flush—Seven Pot red in pepper terms. "Your volcanoes spout mud? One meter in the air? Mud bubbles? Terrible mud bubbles?" Then he began laughing, a hearty wholesome sound of merriment, an infectious glee made sweeter by sharing.

And Vivion found himself braying staccato cackles as he appreciated the silliness of his ridiculous comparison.

They had taken a right turn that led them out to Fifth avenue, right to a vendor selling bottled cold water. They bought two. Vivion insisted on paying. Hideo added 'thank you' to his brief, gracious nod. Then they headed up the avenue. Just as their meandering footsteps, their conversation went here and there, swinging and swaying as they strolled. Until it got back to geography and Vivion opined that although Trinidad clearly was, maybe Tobago was not a part of the South American extended shelf.

Hideo disagreed. Patient and politely, he began, "No. No. No. Not so. It has to be—" and proceeded to give Vivion an informed lesson on Plate Tectonics and how the theory explains relationships between fault lines and subduction and earthquakes and, in his country, Japan, man's eco-sensitive land use and construction of simple, efficient, earthquake-proof homes . . .

Vivion's mind was saying "Whew!" from striving to stay afloat in the data stream. Then like a life line came the mention of homes. Now he too, could show off some expertise. "I'll back you up on efficient houses," he interrupted. "I built one that's completely self-sufficient and I live in it."

Hideo gasped and looked sharp at Vivion. "Really!" he said, "That's awesome!"

"Which is also true," agreed a satisfied Vivion. "I think my house is the first of its kind in the country, a true, true original. I mean in terms of being the first totally self-sufficient regarding electric power. In fact, right now I'm trying to get permission to pass my excess wattage onto the general grid."

His all-ears look appealing for more, Hideo whispered, "Awesome! Amazing. How did . . . ?"

So Vivion gave vent, opened his heart about his dream house and how he had built this personal palace just the way it was conceived. He spoke of his initial inspiration for matters ecological: Dr. Kenny, his ecology professor at university. He recounted how some five years ago he read about a trend for small houses to reduce one's carbon footprint; a trend that had innovative engineers designing small scale power generators such as wind mills, hydro-electric systems, more efficient solar panels and batteries. He went on about how the swift stream snaking through his gardens influenced his vision as energy resource and irrigation.

Throughout the lengthy discourse, an impressed Hideo spurred him on with exclamations of "Wow!" and "Neat" and his seeming favorite, "Awesome!"

Also throughout the monolog it never crossed Vivion's mind to mention his mother's contributions to making the dream palace happen: her essential assists like getting building materials, contracting workmen, importing equipment, signing the paychecks, and so forth.

Dusk was pulling down shades on the bright fall day when they found themselves on Central Park West in the eighties, heading uptown. How they got there, where the hours went, they never knew, but now alert to time and location, hunger was growling for attention. Without mentioning it, Vivion realized he was but a few blocks away from his hostel and the bodega around the corner that he favored. So he suggested they try Latin-flavored Caribbean fare for dinner.

Hideo agreed with the caveat that this time he paid. What else to do. With the condition that he chose their order, Vivion agreed.

From the scant expertise of his stay at the hostel, Vivion had tried a few of the bi-lingual menu's choices. Of them the closest to his Trinidadian tastes was Stewed Chicken with Rice and Beans (*Pollo Guisado con Arroz y Habichuelas*). With Hideo looking on and studying the Spanish translations Vivion ordered it for main course, added a side of boiled Cassava (*Yucca*), and a medium Plain Salad (*Ensalada Mediana*). For beverages he got a Mamey milkshake (*batida de Lechoza*) for Hideo and a Passion Fruit Juice (*Parcha*) for himself. As the waiter, who double-jobbed as cook, turned to return to his domain, Vivion asked, "Señor! Can I get some of your special hot sauce?"

"*No problemo*," said the busy man.

Five minutes later they had their dinners spread before them. What was best hot, steaming so. What was best cool had condensation bubbles teary outside the containers.

Hideo liked the meal well enough, but what he really went for was the hot sauce. And although it made him sweat profusely, he put repeat splashes on his yucca and his rice-and-beans. Partway through the meal, after a cooling sip of Mamey milkshake, he asked Vivion if he would please ask the cook for the recipe. Vivion demurred, "I can't do that, yu'know. Everybody so jealous about they formula, I think I'd embarrass him."

Hideo sopped his forehead with his handkerchief and nodded, "I see, I see. That's true. Forgive me, I am not thinking. A flavor like this would be great hit at our restaurant in Kumamoto City—"

Stung by Hideo's obvious discomfort, Vivion interrupted, "Listen, man! I could give you a recipe that even better than this. Not saying that this here not great. Is just that mine even greater. Is what my mother used to give she *maccomeres*, I mean, like, her best friends. I grow up eating many, many versions of this and I telling you true, every one was special. You want it, I'll give you that recipe."

"You will?" said Hideo, his eager face shining as he withdrew a small black notebook from an inner jacket pocket.

"Yep!" said Vivion, "you ready?"

Hideo nodded, and Vivion closed his eyes to remember better and said, "This is for about a half pint a' sauce. You could always adjust ingredients and quantities to yuh taste. But this is the basics. You need about six, seven ripe hot peppers, Scotch Bonnet or Habañero or varieties like that; add half a teaspoon of salt; a quarter cup of white wine vinegar; three leaves of Shadom Benni, or else you could use a quarter cup of chopped cilantro; crush in two garlic cloves; a couple slices of green papaya, though you could do without this; a small bitter melon, what we does call corrily; slice up half a fresh lemon without the seeds and put that in; and last ingredient, the juice of two ripe limes. I does add a table spoon or two of Greek yogurt, for thickness."

"Anything else?"

"Nah! That's about it. Of course, you make your preferred adjustments. Like you could keep the pepper seeds in for more heat. Leave them out for less. You could add some chop up carrots to balance the pepper heat. You could add more or less vinegar to vary the thickness. That's up to you. Now the last stage is how you mixing it. So you pour everything in a blender and bring it to a smooth slurry, just how you like. Then depending on how regular you using, store yuh sauce in fridge or cupboard. As I said, depending. Oh! Sometimes I does put in some homemade mustard."

"That's it?" asked Hideo.

"Yep! That's how you make pepper sauce like you won't believe! That is until you actually do! No joke!" Vivion smiled a broad one and spread his arms wide, said, "What can I say?" aware that he had made no mention of essential experiences: like how to flavor with local herbs; or if and when to blanch the peppers, or add sugar, curry, or even olive oil. Not a worry to Vivion though. He had given the honest basics, more than enough to show sincerity. Maybe enough to establish trust.

Hideo used his damp handkerchief to pat his face, then blow his nose. "If your recipe makes anything like this, I will be most happy," he said and reached his open hand across the table.

"Well, mih man. I saying straight out right here and now, that you have a tsunami of happiness cruising your way," replied Vivion as he shook the warm, moist hand.

As they walked south alongside the Park towards Hideo's hotel, Vivion said, "So listen, man. I going home this weekend. But I want to give you a special invite to Trinidad, to my home, to my palace. And I hope you don't deny me that honor and privilege."

As was his way, Hideo stopped walking and turned to Vivion. "You are so kind to me. Already I have Trinidad on my itinerary, so it would be no problem for me to visit your special house, your palace home—"

"Not visit," Vivion cut in, "I mean stay. You have to stay by me while you in Trinidad."

"But—"

"No ifs or buts, partner" said Vivion. "I insist. And this has nothing to do with business. Business talk's up to you. Truth is, I just want to show off mih house. So indulge me. Please."

As he considered the offer, Hideo started them walking again, though a bit more slowly. Then he said, "Vivion Pinheiro, I will be honored to stay at your home."

Vivion clapped him on the shoulder, said, "Bet! So it's settled. Email me your arrival and I pick you up at Piarco."

"Yes, Vivion Pinheiro. I will email."

They walked in silence for half a block then as they passed a park bench Hideo said, "I would not mind if you leave me here. I want to sit and think. This is okay I hope."

"Sure, man. Is alright. I should be heading back anyhow. Got stuff to take care of. Did I say I'm leaving Sunday? Well that's the fact. Sunday night coming yuh boy homeward bound."

They both reached out and clasped hands strong and long and comfortable. "I will email," said Hideo.

"Don't forget to stay nice," said Vivion as he turned and headed back uptown, leaving his prospective business partner, granting him thinking space.

When Vivion got to the hostel he used the facilities to email Nikki: Sweetheart. Be home this Monday a.m. Missed you for so much love.

Then he had a hot shower and went to sleep working at not analyzing his good mood, not putting it on his mind at all.

ooOoo

THE LAST FEW DAYS, TUESDAY to Saturday morning, went in a blur, Vivion ticking off assignments he had promised himself if ever the time was right. So one day he took the eight avenue A train to 168th street, to an armory, a place where a decade ago, he won silver in an under-17 four-hundred. He recognized the building by its robust walls' distinctive reddish hue, and for the first time realized that the complex of buildings on adjacent blocks was part the world-famous New York Presbyterian Hospital.

Later on, returned to the hostel unaccountably homesick, he went to the round-the-corner bodega and had a meal of stewed oxtails (*Rabo Guisado*) and rice and beans (*Arroz y Habichuelas*). Although self-conscious of mispronouncing oxtails, he ordered in Spanish, and when the waiter used the menu as a hand to applaud and say, "*Muy bueno, senor. Muy bueno!*" the jolt of pleasure Vivion felt would have surprised Dr. Richter's scale.

Then after a satisfactory dinner he went to sleep around

nine.

Another day, he revisited Macy's for a post-Labor Day sale, bought two pairs of size thirteen for forty-six US dollars—one, except for the swoosh, was a plain black high-top, the other, maybe to compensate for its unappealing design, boasted a thick sole and material that breathed. Still, because their size allowed his wide feet to spread comfortably when shod, this purchase was a bargain.

Then one midday, they were downstairs old-talking when Rawlston John mentioned how the Richmond Hill stop in Queens on the A train would let him out to biggest market place of Caribbean foods and delicacies in the world. "Man, if ah lie ah die," he insisted. "You go find stuff there you can't find back home. They have stewed agouti. In coconut milk. They have jerk pork belly, just off the fire. They have roti, doubles, and phulourie. They have saltfish fritters, accra, and black pudding. You ask in the right place and could get fat fried bake with aloo choka filling . . ."

Like squirrel with peanut butter, Trinis could never resist home food. So sucker to the mouth-watering bait, Vivion took an A train at eighty-six street, and after a long enough ride it never stopped at any station named Richmond Street—and Vivion was looking sharp. So giving up the wild goose chase, he tapped a young fellow's shoulder to get his attention and asked, "Excuse me, sir. You know how I could reverse direction and head back to Manhattan?"

The fellow pulled an earplug from his left ear, said

brusquely, "One stop after this next one," then replaced the attachment to his preferred world.

Two stops and a cross-walk over to the Manhattan bound train, Vivion passed the wait time studying the large posted transit map. After a bit he found the A line and traced it from 86th street, and how you don't know? There was a Richmond Hill stop he had passed several stops ago. But how could he? He puzzled over the question for a while until, just as the train approached his station, the answer came to him.

Richmond Street Boys E.C was the school he attended as a child and that was what he had been looking for—a Richmond Street station, not a Richmond Hill.

Thankfully, Rawlston John was not at the front desk when a frustrated and embarrassed Vivion got back to the hostel, and deciding against dinner, took what comfort he could from a warm shower and the skimpy mattressed single bed.

Five o'clock next afternoon as he registered out of the hostel, Vivion hugged Rawlston John, tipped him an enveloped twenty and bantered, "You have first dibs when I hit the lottery."

And from the good fellow, "Well, I ent waiting, Brother! Safe travels 'til next time!"

After a smooth ride over the bridge and a few miles further, the taxicab was now crawling through traffic for a minute or so then stopping altogether. Vivion asked the driver, "You think we'll make it in time?"

The pale-skinned, unshaven fellow chewed on the toothpick hanging from his lips for a moment before responding. "What time's your flight?" he asked.

"Ten thirty," said Vivion, taking away thirty minutes from the truth for safety. Traffic had stopped the cab again.

"Ten thirty? Which airline you on?" said Driver, doubt in his glance back at Vivion.

"I'm with Com Ex," said Vivion.

"Com Ex, eh. Didn't know they'd gone commercial."

"They didn't," said Vivion improvising, "I work for them."

"Ah. Nice gig. Guess you fly free, huh?"

"Yeah. But they have a limit per month."

The traffic had opened up somewhat and their speed was steadily improving. "So expected!" said Driver, "You just can't beat the white collars."

"I don't aim to beat. I aim to join them bad boys," said Vivion.

Which tickled the driver to chuckle, say, "Can't say I blame yer." The speedometer was now fixed on fifty miles per hour.

Vivion listened to the susurrus of tires on smooth asphalt and wanting more of the relaxing sound, lowered the window. Then the rush of air suggesting, he asked, "What time is it? Please."

"Going on ten-ten and we're five, six minutes from the gates. You got lotsa time," said the driver.

Vivion leaned back in his seat and relaxed. He did have lotsa time.

He walked into the passengers area, looked at a big clock on the second balcony and saw it was ten twenty. He moved to a chair that gave him vantage to the clock and sat down. After a bit, he opened his backpack, removed pertinent documents and stowed them in the inner breast pocket of his shirt jacket. He closed his eyes and leaned his head on the wall behind the chair.

Time passed as myriad thoughts mobbed his mind. Hideo Arata and common business interests vs. Nikki and everything she was to him vs. Rawlston Johnny and his comfortable position vs. Mother's reaction to all that had happened vs. the guy Lambkin and his odd scent vs. Spoon and Jeanette and their beautiful children Vivion had missed seeing vs. . . .

"Stop!" Vivion murmured to himself, opened his eyes and glanced at the clock on the upper balcony.

And there in all whites, lounging casual against the banister and seeming to look directly at Vivion, was Tommy Tyson.

Vivion waggled a hand at him, swung the back-pack up on his shoulder and started for the escalator to the upper floor.

Tommy met him as he stepped off the escalator, stuck out his hand. "Gimme some flesh," he said with a broad smile, and looking handsome as any six-foot-six, two hundred-twenty pound aircraft captain would.

They shook hands. Held on strong, lingering comfortably as only true friends can. Then Tommy said, "Well, let's do it. Earlier is better 'round this joint."

"I'm down with that, mih Brother," agreed Vivion.

Then they were off to deal with the bureaucracy of international travel.

Smooth as a breeze, no problems at all, they were in the air at five after eleven. And despite all the excitements provoking his mind Vivion was sanguine all the way home.

He made himself a long thin bed by raising the hand-rests of a row of seats. Then comfortable on the pallet, Vivion allowed his thoughts to wander onto his piece of paradise, his gently sloping twenty-acre plot of land that used to be part of a failed cocoa estate . . .

Shaped roughly like a resting butterfly with wings spread wide, it was divided by a tributary of the Ortoire river, a swift stream that occasionally pooled to sandy-bottomed basins perfect for bathing. All the cocoa trees had been bulldozed away to form landfill, or be made into charcoal. Now, on the wooded side, here and there tall red-flowered immortelle trees stood casting skinny shadows, sighing to the breezes and swaying like mourners. Nearer to earth, dark-green leaved Tonka bean trees lent special fragrance to the air.

A charming sylvan piece of ground, it was.

After learning what were his majors in University, Mother had bought the property in his name. When she gave him the deed as a graduation present, Vivion was indifferent. Although he had no specific other in mind, he was uninterested in agriculture as a career. It sounded like work and schedules, matters anathema to his indolent nature. That he had majored with honors in chemistry and zoology—with a particular interest in ecology—was only because quick learner that he was, these subjects came easiest to him.

The chapter of his life upon graduating could have been entitled 'Chasing Feckless Fun!' Reckless shenanigans, loud parties and promiscuity ruled while his Missus Pinheiro fumed. As bleary mornings followed hard-used nights, when ever he got to the kitchen for food, Mother would be there complaining, "Yuh behavior ruining mih reputation after I work so hard to repair it."

"You is a shameless lout, Vivion, a disgrace to yuh family name!"

"Why you don't look at yuh self, eh. A gadabout wastrel is how you intend to use yuh fancy education?"

Her barrages continued right through Christmas, carnival, cricket season - January to May - and well into the rainy season. Then she objected to a planned party during *petit carême*, and Vivion lost his temper, spoke his mind: "You're a nag, Mother! You killing me with yuh constant complaining! You depressing mih moods. I have a life to live. I young and strong and need to make mih memories, good or bad I don't care. Memories, Mother. I have to live *my* life! I can't let you stop me!"

At that, the kitchen developed an intense quiet. All at once he could hear the outside. Yard chickens peeping and mother hens clucking. Birds cheeping in the guava tree. While there in the kitchen, bakes sizzled in the frying pan and Mother pronounced, "Well Mister Man. I can't have you living this kind of life under *my* roof! I cannot and will not let you carry on with this worthless behavior. You hearing me, Mister Vivion? So is either you change yuh ways, or you change address! You hearing me?"

Not only hear, but Vivion could see in her face the resolve. This was it. He was at a crossroads. Moreover, he knew just as well that he had no option but to yield. Yet this was also when Vivion got the first thought of having his own place.

So for peace and commonsense purpose, he modified his ways, and though stung by the notion of changing address, the choice of location was a no-brainer: he'd use the land she bought him.

Loosely middling the property, the gurgling creek with big rocks and lively water snaked along off and on eddying into clear pools that invited 'come on in and splash'. Mainly because it slowed down along the belly of a long curve the bank of which seemed an ideal picnic spot, the creek was the resource on the property to first interest him. Beyond the major attraction of being very far away from the bungalow and his mother's displeasure, other conveniences were its pools of chest-deep, sparkling water; and, right down to the stream's edge, innocuous flowering bushes that craved for attention from a thrown blanket; and, if circumstances should require shade and privacy, a dense copse of wild breadfruit trees that offered same.

Indeed, as a party spot it was second to none.

But when Vivion thought in terms of changing address, it was an even more ideal location for a house. Thirty meters from the creek, the slight slope flattened out to open sunlit space for another fifty or so, more than enough to put up a good-sized building. A three, four bedroom, or even a two-storied four-bedroom house. A house in a fertile spot favored by shading fruit trees, more of which he would plant.

Yes! In his mind's eye, everything was right and ready, and his favorite picnic spot was longing for a house. As the year-end holidays approached, he'd go to the land and stand looking around, daydreaming ideas for his house-to-be, its conveniences and utilities. Then one day his ecology studies butted into his fancies and the creek's slightly zigzag course set him thinking of energy—its flow, its rushing sound, its control and capture for irrigation and electric power.

Then in a fever from these ideas and still having his student identification, he visited the University to look for his favorite teacher.

Dr. Kenny was the biology professor at UWI. Trini-born white, he was a passionate nature-lover, kept humming-bird feeders all around his cottage in Maracas hills, made sourdough bread from homegrown wild yeast. He made biology fun, made it live. In his classes, you wanted more. One of his pedagogic innovations was to separate the course into three areas—zoology, botany, and ecology—with ecology having equal value in final exams.

Another was learning from and in the field. There, his favorite students had the privilege to call him Kenny, no title. Which was huge. Every ambitious student, the girls more blatant than the boys, competed at sucking up to him. Although Vivion didn't slave at it, he was up there among the topmost. Kenny's teaching turned him on to ecology. The result? As was his way, Vivion read more widely than necessary, and more than most, learned to juggle theory, fact, and consequence. Most significantly, he saw the basic interdependence of the various manifestations of a vibrant holistic Nature.

Kenny as his muse, Vivion aced every test.

Talking about field experiences, this was Kenny: Sold to them as a Sunday morning hike, he had most of the class sweating and panting up the trails of El Cerro del Aripo, at close to thirty-one hundred feet, the highest mountain peak in Trinidad. Finally at the top, the fellas, in shorts and t-shirts, were soon chilled out of the fun. The girls, more sensibly garbed in slacks and long sleeves to protect their skin, took many cozy pictures of their achievement.

Meanwhile Kenny, breeze flapping baggy trousers about his bony legs, strode about the observation area smiling broadly, declaiming to no one in particular, "Look at this view. Isn't it magnificent? Tell me. Tell me now. Now isn't it grand? Look at this magnificence."

Another time Kenny had a brave, or reckless, dozen souls crawling down into the bowels of the earth to study bat caves, and by the by, forever imprint on their consciousness the disgusting experience of wading ankle-deep through horrible, stinking bat-shit on which mouse-sized cockroaches gorged.

Then twice each year, Kenny took his class to beaches of Balandra where, moonlight or no, endangered turtles journey in from worlds away to lay their eggs. Sixty, seventy days later, for up to seven nights, hundreds of thousands of hatchlings will burrow out of their sand covered nests and scramble down the beach through a gauntlet of greedy predators, heading for the sea and a life of unimaginable hazards. The hundred or so that mature will then undertake the same arduous journey for the rest of their amazing lives.

One night, on the way back from the leatherbacks of Balandra, Kenny showed them a part of the Ortoire river where the water in the deeper bathing basins glowed blue to green on dark nights after a day of hot sunshine. Vivion jumped in the water and, for long instants, the splashes reminded him of the sparkle of a micro Milky Way. Was truly breathtaking.

For the field trip to end second-year biology, Kenny and his assistant, Dr. Price, took thirteen of the top students to the out-back of Guyana to live with primal natives for three mind-opening weeks; an amazing adventure for Vivion that also brought him closer to his classmates. Especially when he stripped to jockey shorts to really experience the day-to-day of the native men.

Then after two days of insect bites and stings and buzzings; and native young men slapping his chest to see the hand imprints appear bright red then fade away; and children crowding around him to measure themselves against his impressive height. Plus, on the second day just before sun set, when he realized that he had a quiet, hidden audience while at the creek bathing away his day's grime and sweat. Persuaded by these accumulated experiences, the third morning he returned to civilized clothes, and continued to learn from those inquisitive natives.

Though it was approaching two in the afternoon, class time, Vivion took the chance and knocked on Dr. Kenny's office door.

"Come in," came the familiar energetic tenor.

Cheering himself for trying, Vivion entered, greeted, "How you doing, Doc?" and stuck out his hand.

Kenny enclosed the hand in a warm, bony grip with both of his and shook it. "How's it with you, young Pinheiro. How is it? How is it?" Same old repeat-himself-as-emphasis Kenny.

"I'm doing great, sir. Was in the neighborhood and thought I'd look you up. See if you still around."

"Well, I'm that, and plan to be a sizeable bit more. Yes sir, that's my plan, my boy. Ha-ha-ha. What's yours? Ha-ha-ha. Eh?"

Kenny was a thin fellow about six feet tall, a little less than forty years old, and balding prematurely. His high, prominent forehead put one in mind of the Bard. But although Kenny was a specially intelligent man, it was his plain *joie-de-vivre* in pursuit of ecological subtleties that set him apart as a lecturer. Vivion always liked chatting with him. "Well," he said, "these days I'm looking for an affordable low tech hydroelectric system that would work in a creek. I'm thinking about building a house up in the country where they don't have electricity yet. But the land have a creek on it. So the idea is to create enough energy to power the household electric requirements."

Kenny was enthusiastically supportive. "Most interesting, young Pinheiro. Very nice, indeed," said he as he used a cigarette lighter to fire up his cold pipe. "Most interesting. Fact is, just recently, what? Two weeks ago? I read something quite relevant. It was in that American eco-zine, you know, put out by . . . Ahhh!" he sucked hard on the pipe-stem and rocked his narrow torso forward and backwards in an effort to rouse his memory. But just as when Vivion took the professor's lectures, Recall remained stubborn and/or drowsy.

Partly to revive the conversation, Vivion asked, "When you say relevant, the equipment, the machine they showed, was it dependable? You think it'd work down here?"

"Yes, yes. This system is ideal for tropic use. In fact, any environment with free flowing water would do. Of course, the swifter the better. Ha-ha-ha. Yes, yes. They currently use it in Columbia. So yes, I think it'd certainly meet your needs."

Vivion nodded. "Good, very good. Very good," he said and smiled a quick one partly because, unconsciously, he had imitated Kenny's speaking pattern. He continued, "What I have in mind is a two-story house with Plexiglas walls and eight rooms. Well, actually four bedrooms with adjoining bathrooms, and two spacious all included living, cooking, dining, and lounging areas on either floor. At every perimeter, tall, flimsy, white curtains would give privacy."

"Sounds wonderful. Wonderful indeed. Where you putting up this magnificent structure?"

"Well, I have a few acres going up Tamana way. The land flat and slightly sloped to meet near the middle where it have a nice creek running through."

"Sounds like it should also have a steady breeze moving up or down them Tamana hills, huh?"

"Now you mention it, that might actually be the case, you know."

"Then I have another idea for you. What about you double up energy-wise by getting a small windmill or two? What about that? Like those they use on recreational vehicles. Hmmn! What you think? I should check that out as well, eh. What you think?"

Vivion enthused, "Oh, Doc. That'd be great. Just fantastic. Neat."

Then Kenny looked at his watch and asked. "You have the time?"

Vivion who never carried a watch said, "No," but right away understood the situation. He had over stayed his welcome and made Kenny late for his lecture. "Look, Doc," he said, "I'm cruising, okay. Get back to you in a few. Next week? Thanks for all them ideas. Is what I was hoping for. Really. So thanks again." He stuck out his hand to shake, and Kenny paused a moment from gathering folders to complement the gesture.

Then Vivion was out of there.

It was a month before Kenny came through. He called inviting Vivion to his office and showed him magazines with manufacturers advertising energy storage machines, and energy conversion machines, and miniature windmills. There were details of strengths and weaknesses, applicability and delivery options, promises of reliable service in person or on video, and at the bottom of all the explanatory diagrams and nice pictures, shipping costs.

All he could wish for to electrify his dream house.

Then a few days later, at ease on the back verandah

enjoying a cool afternoon, Vivion brought up the subject. "Mother," he said, "what you think of a self-supporting house that have its own electricity? I mean self-sufficient regarding air-conditioning, and fridge, and stove, and so forth. Eh? What you think?"

"Sounds like a good idea. You talking solar, no?"

"As only part of the supply. We could use hydroelectric and wind energy, too."

Mother chuckled, asked, "You mean tiny Dutch windmills?"

"Ent no joke, Mother. People does use them already for their recreational vehicles. You'd be surprised how much energy them li'l windmills could provide."

"Well, boy, I all for it. Unless you thinking a' putting up windmill on *this* bungalow, because then the answer is a definite No! I want mih house stay how it be."

"Nah, Mother. Not at all. I thinking of a modern fresh-built house with wide, gradual, wraparound inclined verandahs instead of stairs between the two floors. Each floor would have a kitchen, bathrooms, bedrooms. Well, maybe only the ground floor will have a kitchen. The rooftop will have a thousand gallon storage water tank equipped with hard water filters, and on the side of the house away from the river, a five-hundred gallon tank on the ground from which collected water from the roof's extra-wide Plexiglas eves would be pumped back up to the rooftop tank for filtration, chemical adjustment, and storage. That way the taps in the bathrooms and kitchens would gush hot or cold, hard or soft, clean—"

Mother put a hand up and stopped him. A small smile

supporting the twinkle in her eyes, she said, "Okay, you losing me. But I getting the picture of a house. You, we, been planning this for a while, eh?"

Vivion blushed, realized that he might have overspoken. "Yes, Mammy, yuh boy's been thinking of putting up a house. A special house. A—"

Amused, Mother cut in, "—self-sufficient house that would be a marvel of innovation. You repeating yuh self, boy. Now tell me straight! What you getting at?"

So Vivion took his time and expounded on his dreamhouse. Where it'd be, and how it'd look with its Plexiglas walls built around steel stanchions anchored in six-foot deep concrete trenches, and how it'd have four or five foot wide eaves for collecting rain like ancient Chinese grand houses did . . .

And his mother smiled all the while he rhapsodized. For this dreamer was the child she adored. His outbursts of ideas, some with points of brilliance like stars that blinked brighter in a night's sky. All of this reminded her of one other and made every consequence worthwhile. Right then she was the luckiest mother in the world as Vivion imaged and presented his eccentric countryside castle for her approval. Thrilled by his enterprise, enthusiastic to make it happen, already her business head was thinking practical. Her wealth made financing no problem, and in any case, she'd get good returns on her outlay by selling three or four acres at the farthest end of the property—not right then, but later on when, with an attraction like Vivion's famous self-sustaining mansion, they'd go like hops bread hot from the oven.

So three swift months later, with Tommy Tyson helping as the major transport connection, Mother bought and had the necessary energy equipment brought into the country, and electricity arrangements were a done deal.

Then it was the actual construction process; the routine of the drawing up architectural plans, hiring contractors, getting the specialized materials like Plexiglas and treated bamboo for the floors, and the rubberized carpet for the inclines, and a hundred other minor essentials, and finally the building of the structure. None of it true hurdle, all needed to make it happen was currying, or calling in, some favors.

As usual, taking care of it all, she'd be her efficient, dependable self for her one-and-only.

With house construction progressing satisfactorily, Andaluza never stopped being a guiding, caring, forceful mother. So she pestered and prodded until, one blazing hot day she got Vivion to explain his afore-mentioned intentions for the land. They had crossed the creek to sit on a rock at its edge and cool their feet in the sparkling water while watching the busy crews work. "Tell me about it," said Mother.

"Is like this," he said, "I figure that once the house finish and everything in working order, it could be a long piece a' empty time on mih hands out here in the country. I mean I like the quiet, but with nothing to do! Oy! That's when boredom will start giving courage to chaos. Not the plan for me. So I thinking of starting up a li'l farm. A pepper farm."

"A pepper farm?" echoed Mother, surprise pitching her voice high.

"Well, lemme tell you why. You remember all that excitement about Moruga Red Scorpion winning out as the hottest pepper in the world? Well, that set me thinking. I believe normal people can't eat Moruga Scorpion. It just too hot for enjoyment. So my idea is to create a more appealing, cooler, mass-market hybrid. All it take is basic botany. In UWI yuh boy was aces in biology and I have the genetics o' cross breeding down pat. So I thinking to use about a couple acres for experimenting. Put up a li'l nursery alongside to . . . "

Mother had stopped listening. Excited to see him making use of himself and his fancy education, and on the land, to boot, she was immediately on board. "I could see what you talking. Cross it with coffee pepper," she suggested. "Me. I do like mih pepper the hotter the better. But sometimes cross breeds could be really nice. You musta seen them half-size Peter peppers in mih backyard garden, eh? They is cross breed. Taste real good. too. Zesty. I have six, seven different breeds in that garden for suiting mih day-to-day. Yuh mother just like to indulge she palate with that sweet heat!"

So about his pepper farm proposal, yes, Mother was over the moon.

Right away she was plying him with advice. Necessary wisdoms like: "Don't worry yuh head 'bout financing. I going take care of that, but you have to keep the whole venture within maverick means."

And "Follow yuh research. Learn everything about

anything relating to the business."

And "Be particular about planning production, and choosing varieties, and preparing fields, and nurturing the seedlings. And don't forget planning for disease and how to manage if it hit you. Sterilize and start over? Usually that is best."

As she paused to think up another insight, Vivion exclaimed, "Mother! Where you get all this kinda know-how?"

"Boy! Yuh mother is a successful woman! She's a real estate business baron. And she does make garden in she backyard. So she's a agriculture expert too. Right? Bottom line, when she want to know something, yuh mother does talk to any and everybody who know about it better. She does listen close and she have a spongy brain! So what! You think I only able at building lotsa house and making a smart and extra-long mix-breed son?" she replied proudly.

Good moods further boosted, she went on to urge that he listen to the farmers, to the poor fellows who actually worked the land. "They have success knowledge," she explained. "But you have to learn how to listen to them. To hear what they saying. They don't always say it right, but remember they trying. If they trust you with their own ways of saying something, they going try harder to make you understand. They going teach you their language. You got to work and catch it because they more proud when the two efforts win out and you gain their knowledge. These be the fellas you want around you. Higher the best of them. Pay them well. Be generous when they go off kilter and mess up. Forgive they mistakes. Laugh and punish them with a day off with pay. You do that and they'd work day or night, sun and rain, sick or hale for you because you done thief respect from they souls."

Vivion only objection was, "Mother, you didn't have to put it so. Saying I stole they souls. You coulda say win. I win they souls from them." But his tone had wink in it. Which really made all the difference because from his eyes beamed absolute admiration.

ooOoo

NIKKI HAD WANTED TO ASK the question when it first occurred to her, but didn't because it would've interrupted Ramiya's telling. Almost every day since then it had crossed her mind: after how he mistreated her, what moved Andaluza to build the house for Vivion?

So she decided to get to the bungalow a little before noon time when she knew Andaluza would be out doing her business and Ramiya'd be home alone. She called Dylan Taxis, asked for Aaqilah Madani to pick her up at eleven; extra early as she had planned a special treat for Ramiya.

Aaqilah was prompt and after a short detour, got Nikki to the bungalow ten minutes before noon. They arranged for Aaqilah to return at five and Nikki climbed the twenty flat steps, pressed the buzzer and Ramiya soon opened the door and welcomed her in.

She followed Ramiya into the kitchen where, from the delicious aroma, Nikki realized that she had interrupted a making of sour-sop ice cream. "Oh gosh!" she cried, "you know this is mih favorite of all ice cream? I know you sharing. Right?"

"What else you think? Luz like it too. Is just that I wasn't expecting you so early."

Nikki remembered her surprise and pulled a tall gift-wrapped box from her oversize handbag and proffered it to Ramiya dramatically saying, "For you, milady!"

Ramiya drew back her head and looked up at Nikki, her raised eyebrows skeptical while a pleased smile played at her mouth. "What is that?" she asked.

Grinning hugely, Nikki said, "Open it and find out."

Ramiya stopped stirring the ice cream slurry, thoroughly wiped her hands in her skirt tails, and took the box. She put it on the table and carefully undid the knot of a large blue ribbon bow. Then, wrapping paper removed and the contents exposed, Ramiya's face went surprised and something less readily defined. "You bring that for me?" she asked almost testily. "Why, that's the best brandy they have. It cost a fortune. I don't know what to say. I mean I appreci—"

Nikki cut in, "Just say thanks, Ramiya. Not even that, because truth is you deserve the best because you *is* the best." She moved in and hugged the buxom woman feeling a bit manipulative as she thought of her primary intent.

A little later, after Ramiya was done with prepping her ice cream slurry and setting it to churn in the electric machine, she brought two glasses from the cupboard and suggested, "So let we break the seal, nuh."

That put Nikki in a small dilemma. Not primarily because her father was a strict Muslim, she generally avoided alcohol. A sip of white wine now and then was her limit. But knowing what she had in mind, it seemed really gauche to say no to a drink right then. So with a laugh, she said, "Just a sip for me. I don't have much resistance and I don't want you taking me home."

"Girl, I don't blame you," said Ramiya, smiling like an imp as she barely splashed the bottom of Nikki's tall glass and halved her own, "is a seductive habit but a bad one. Though is okay for pagan me. I don't have no Hell to go to."

Still, in a little bit of time, the sip was sufficient to shift the purpose of her visit from Nikki's immediate mind. And with dry corn already fine-grated in the mixing bowl, and seasoned meat ready for broiling, and banana leaves cut to size, Ramiya insisted on showing off her version of making chicken pastels.

Nikki didn't mind at all, as gradually, she found herself fuzzily fascinated by how Ramiya really enjoyed her versatile electric mixing bowl.

Guava

ooOoo

As VIVION STEPPED OUT the aircraft's door a warm blast
that stunk of petrol fumes made him gasp. "Is like an air-
conditioner exhaust belching, 'Welcome Home'," observed
captain Tommy Tyson with a laugh. Then they climbed
down the stairs and went to meet the authorities. So shortly
after four in the morning, swift through Immigration and
Customs due to Tommy's influence, Vivion was in a limo
heading for his palace in Serene Valley.

The night was clear, starry-skied, and he felt vigorous,
mind sharp and eager to get on with life. Both passenger
windows levered halfway down, his heart raced as he sucked
in the subtleties of the crisp morning air, relishing its
prompts to memories. He sighed heavily, leaned back into
the soft leather seat and closed his eyes. He wanted to
remember this flavor of feelings borne on breezes from the
black mysterious forests through which the car was passing.
For this was the part of coming home he most loved; this
thrill of reacquainting with the familiar; this opportunity to

see it new and fresh again.

And this time there was added an anticipation above every previous—in a word, Nikki, *his sweet and precious Nikki*! Then at the thought of her, he shot swift guilty eyes at the driver's head as he wiggled his butt to adjust his underwear to better accommodate a sudden erection.

They travel further at night, so Vivion had the limo drop him off some fifty yards from his gate so that sounds of his arrival—the car's engine, the door slammed shut, the wheels crunching on a graveled roadway—would not disturb the peaceful palace. Then, as the transport turned around and returned the way it had come, he ambled through the moonlight towards the gate, cheerfully peering into the close dark forests, trying to identify the various tweets and shrill peeps that sounded from them.

Which was tree-frog? Or night bird? Or cricket? Which was warning? Which was death cry, or just a show-off? What sound did douens make?

Never certain of which or any, he could only ponder.

He punched in the password on the panel and with a quiet *click!* the door unlocked. He slid it open and entered, breathing in deep of this true and perfect scent of Home. He put down his back-pack, and light enough from the bright moon outside, prowled to the fridge, poured himself a glass of fresh cow's milk. He drank it slowly, savoring every swallow, then went to the back bathroom and took a quick quiet hot shower. He toweled dry, and naked as a bird's backside, tiptoed into his study, the place he most lived in, the place his love would be.

Moonbeams through the curtains broke the room into a pattern of soft light and shadow. In a bright part, plain on the night stand at the head of his bed was a bottle of brandy and two glasses, one with a finger of liquor in it.

In a shadowed side of the bed, lay Nikki, *his Nikki*, on her back, lightly snoring welcoming intentions, a pale thin twisted sheet here and there covering her body's varied shades of darkness.

What else to do? Careful not to rouse her, he lay beside her and shifted enough of the sheet over him so that he could gently hug her skin-to-skin close.

ooOoo

IN THE PERIOD THAT FOLLOWED, time went out of synch, lost its measure. They were simply together, touching, holding, laughing, admiring each other like new-found miracles. They washed each other in the showers as if it were never done before. Off and on she'd pull him into the kitchen and make for him a dish she had at the moment dreamed up. Then that might sequence into them tasting each other's offerings.

In a way, everything they did was love making. Even explaining to each other their special connection. Even proposing theories and conclusions about it. Even attributing their notions to this or that philosophy, or religion, or science. Then they laughed at their ideas until their sides and faces actually hurt.

Then through the pain, they laughed at that.

For Vivion it was all sublime. He had read or heard the adage that sophistication is a matter of experience. Now, to that old saw, he could add the wrinkle that a lucky man could learn a decade's worth in days.

Girls and women falling for him was sort of normal—

had been since he became interested. Dependent on how she played the romance game, reacted to his moves, and responded with intellect and body fragrance, he had been as hot for them. Scent was important to him. Sensitive to pheromones, he got a sense of a person's feelings from their smell. The insight was not presented in detail, but it gave indications. Weighted the emotional dice. Helped out Intuition and filled him with confidence—an advantage that he enjoyed, or maybe was dependent upon.

With Nikki he never needed that edge. From the very first he met her, by much, much more than aroma, he knew she was for him. It was a special intense nature of her intimacy. She spoke her heart and made it a song. When inevitably, they got together, making love was effortless and mutually satisfying. Now since his return somehow she was different. A subtle, superior different. In some mysterious way, intangibles had changed.

It used to be that her manner during a love tussle was at the same time defiant surrender, reluctant appeal preceding command, then breathless competition to a finish. He had learned to accept her eyes rolling upwards during climax, the whites bare—an ecstasy that was at first frightening as it was flattering. Now a new tenderness had entered the equation. Sometimes her gleaming eyes on him were contemplative as if studying for portraits. And as only his nose knew, her fondness was more flavorful, like sweet dark chocolate with peppy highlights. Whatever the reason, more than ever before he felt an absolute man, a victor, a lover, a beloved hero come back home.

Smiling shyly at each other, they returned to normal earth that Wednesday afternoon and after a test run of the new reality, Vivion asked her to walk with him among the peppers while she brought him up to date with what went down during his absence. Nikki clasped her hands together and shoved her skirt between her legs and rocked her shoulders sideways like a playful preteen and said in singsong, "Only if you hold my hand . . . " A wussy practice at which he never indulged.

"No problem, sweetheart," agreed Mr. Lover supreme. Perhaps so because their affair had attained such a lofty level.

Outside, *petite carême* was near to the end of its six week reign and the sun was exaggerating its abilities. Daily temperatures hovered over mid thirties, Celsius. Today Wednesday was no different. At around three o'clock, Vivion shut down his computer, leaned back on his chair and stretched mightily. He got up, cast a dispirited look at the brightness outside and headed for the fridge. From the bed Nikki said, "Glass a' milk for yuh darling?"

He poured her milk and fixed a half-and-half of brandy and coconut water for himself. Took the drinks back to the study, gave Nikki hers, resumed his seat and sipped and stared out at the hot world.

Nikki came and stood beside him, put an arm around his neck and kissed his cheek. "Why we don't chill in the house while I bring you up to date with everything," she suggested.

"Every thing?" said Vivion.

"Yes, that too!"

So that's just what they did.

Later on, sitting side by side backs against the headboard, somewhat disconcerted at her familiarity with his mother, Vivion listened as Nikki told of Andaluza's visit to her parents, specifying with a wagging forefinger that the story was exactly as Andaluza related it to her.

So they're now 'Andaluza' close! thought Vivion. What happened here?

"Is no profit for me here, okay," said Nikki, "Ah selling as ah buying. In truth it started with a question she ask the previous time I went by. Maybe the second or third visit. I wasn't making memory notes like somebody we know."

She elbowed his ribs as an exclamation point and went on. "Is only afterwards that I realize the question wasn't so innocent as she put it. What she ask was, 'How you and yuh parents getting on these days?' And before I could even answer, she follow up with, 'You know you have to make up with them, eh!' saying it like it was written by the Moving Finger.

"And that's what get me hot. That finality attitude. It change me from dismissing the matter to defending mih self. So I put it to she right away. I point out that it was *them* who spit *me* out. Is *them* who bearing grudge and feeling shame. When I tried to explain mih self to *them*, is Babu who slam down he coffee on the kitchen table walk out. So as far as I concern, is not Shanika Grant-Ali who have to make up with anybody.

"Andaluza come back with, 'So in a way you doing exactly what they expect, eh?'

"'What you mean?' I say.

"'Well, look at it their way. They know you and yuh stubbornness. You most likely get that from yuh father. So he, at least, know you not changing yuh mind. What you have to realize now is that with how you acting, they don't have no knowledge of yuh real, actual situation. They don't know if you happy or sad or shame or being abused by my vagabond man-child. By now they must have picked up gossip about him and he *vi-que-vi* ways. So all yuh parents doing now is worry about the future of their only one remaining. You don't think so?'

"Well, Vivion, your darling ent that easy. I give Andaluza some more facts. I point out that I know who wasn't thinking what she thinking. Because I know mih mammy was not. She not strong-willed. She'll go along with anything Babu say and that's the problem. Like every Muslim man, Babu always wanted a boy child, and when Ahmed pass he get vex with he world and he god and he everything. Imagine Babu, an imam, didn't mention the Hajj for years. Worst than that, with he boy-child dead, all he had left was this girlchild who don't take orders, and who he going have to marry off with dowry one day.

"So then he run away to New York and everything change up side down. Mammy open she roti shop and I get scholarship because I had talent. Talent, I point out to Andaluza, that woulda never get notice home down here.

"That was yuh girl going on, speaking mih mind, letting it out, when Andaluza stick she hand up like when she have a point to make. So I look at she and let mih face say 'What?'

"She ups up with, 'You should never go hard on a mother. You don't know what she might be going through. It have quiet mothers that don't say much. But when they talk you should listen. Because what they saying is like rubies, formed from blood and pressure. Lemme tell you something nobody ent know. When mih father decided to move we here, he didn't tell mih mother he plans, but the night before we leave, Ashaki slip quiet, quiet to mih bed and gimme a mudada doll to protect me. Then in a whisper she tell me that she was going run-way with a Jamaican cane-cutter that same night. She parting words to me was, '*Disobey the rhythm, girl. Dance yuh own dance.*' Small as I was, I never forget that. I still living by that motto.'

"Well, boy. Not only the motto, but that was the first time Andaluza ever mention to me she mother and father in the same breath. Just taking that in, I could hardly talk. I say something stupid like, 'Your mother wise'. Don't even remember. I was so taken aback. I know it kinda shock me out mih own defensiveness. So two days after that I let she take me to visit them."

"Really? You and yuh parents on good terms again?"

"Well, sort of. They still waiting to meet you formally and . . . "

"I don't mind at all," said Vivion, Master of the Moment. "Once Hideo gone back we could set up a date."

"Hideo? Who Hideo?"

"Oh, I ent tell you? Is a fella I meet in New York who coming to visit. A Japanese fella. Is why I want to go look at the peppers. What you think? I sure now cooler outside."

"Darling, I ent going out there, yu'know," said Nikki,

sounding drowsy. "I telling you it just too hot and in here so nice and cool and comfy. Why we don't lie down a li'l bit?"

Vivion looked at his lover, met eyes speaking erotic sign language, sending a stirring invitation he just could not decline.

So they never did leave the palace all that sultry Wednesday.

Awoken by her absence, Vivion reached his arm long over one side of the big bed while he blinked bleary eyes at the other. Yes, Nikki was gone. He passed a palm over the rumpled, twisted bed-sheet and from the coolness figured she was long gone. Maybe awoken by his snores and went to her own bed; she could be touchy sometimes. He sighed and knowing that for him sleep was gone as well, sat up and swung his feet onto the cool bamboo floor. He rubbed his face hard with both palms, stretched until his bones popped, then stood up and went to the fridge. He lifted out a gallon container, put his lips to it and guzzled cold fresh milk.

Back in his study, he turned on the computer and found he had two messages: one from a New York address, the other from HaRaTa.com. Vivion opened the one from Hideo and smiled as he read: Stopped extra day in Antigua. Now flight will arrive at Piarco 7.00 pm on Friday. See you then. Best regards, Hideo Arata.

The second email was from Lambkin & Harris—Importers, Exporters. It read: Dear Mr. Vivion Pinheiro, we at Lambkin & Harris wish to offer you a position as business representative in your country, Trinidad. We have done due diligence regarding your qualifications, initiative, education, and heritage. We believe that you are the ideal person for our future plans. If interested, please respond within the next ten work days. Thank you. Signed, Lambkin & Harris Inc.

As Vivion read the Lambkin & Harris email a complicated smile grew on his face, and it only got wider as he read message again. Then he read it once more, this time critically, unsmiling. First mistake, his country was Trinidad and Tobago. Next was the 'heritage' bit. From what and whom did they get that data? Was it the old guard creoles who identify themselves as Portuguese disrespecting whatever other blood running in their veins? Did his grandfather's name swing the vote his way? Was it that that made him ideal? Finally, so he had ten days, eh! They couldn't wait to own his time! Acting as if already he on their dole?

This thinking setting a mood, he sucked his teeth and clicked the email into 'Saved'. Then he read Hideo's again and a pleasant smile returned.

He tamped his restlessness until dawn when, flashlight in hand, he slipped out of the house and headed to his pepper fields. He walked past the enclosed nursery, continued towards the general beds, flashing the beam on individual plants as with growing dismay, with tree after tree, he found something profoundly amiss.

He straightened up and looked over the darkness of his garden, and faced the fact. It seemed that in his three-week absence the bountiful harvest had disappeared! In all his searching, off and on he'd found a lonely, malformed one stubbornly hanging on. But it was undeniable. The exceptional pepper crop was no more!

He walked past three beds thinking of possibilities. Was it blight? Insect infestation? Water starvation?

But where was the evidence? The flashlight's questing beam revealed no sign of fungi on the trees. No accumulation of sick or fallen peppers on the ground. Neither was the earth parched. So such could not be the causes.

Now he was even more puzzled. What could have happened? The fearsome waste of time and money brought to mind Mother, as an angry scold. He heaved a breath, blew that thought away. What ever happened, though, she'd be the one most likely to know, and with their new familiarity, maybe Nikki did as well. So he gave up on negative speculations and turned back for the house.

Dawn was breaking, the sun peeking golden rays over the forested horizon, promising a sparkling day. It made a cheerful image that did not move Vivion. He entered the house, realized he could smell his own anxiety and headed directly to the shower. He set the faucet to 'hot' and stayed under the stream until his skin was florid and his mind refreshed.

Done and dressed, he went into his study, sat down in his chair frowning at the clock, trying to decide when he'd wake up Nikki for answers.

He waited until eight-thirty before venturing up to her room. As expected, crouched up like a fetus, she was asleep. Vivion stood looking at her, gnawing his bottom lip, working out whether Necessity had made him bold enough to wake her. Negatives winning, he returned to his study and sat fiddling with a pencil. He'd wait until nine o'clock, he decided. Two minutes later he got up and went to the kitchen. Fried two eggs. Slipped them into a sliced coconut bake, added a sliced tomato and with a cup of warm cow's milk to wash the sandwich down, had breakfast. Done with eating, dishes washed and back in his study, it was only ten minutes to nine.

He sat in his chair and pondered how she'd react if awoken by loud music. Suppose it was from one of her soothing favorites, like Lata Mangeshkar. Then he thought of how Lata's high-pitched notes were comparable to opera. A sort of Hindi opera, and sweet though the melodies could be, sometimes those notes in higher reaches did irritate. Irrational, but fact; it happened to him.

Next time Vivion looked at the clock it was ten after nine.

He rushed up the incline to her room. She was still sound asleep. So nothing ventured nothing gained, he sat on the edge of her bed and began to gently massage her foot.

After a minute or so she pulled away the foot and rolled on to her back. Rubbing her eyes with both hands she asked crossly, "What you doing?"

"Waking you. It cool and nice outside. I thought we could stroll down to the creek and . . . " he let the suggestion float unfinished.

Nikki had rolled onto her side turning her back to him. Then she pulled the cover sheet over her head and mumbled, "Vivion, I don't wake up so early." And almost right away she was breathing sleeping-deep again.

Vivion sucked in his bottom lip and worried it with his teeth as he returned to his chair in the study. He thought through possibilities once again. Then hoping against hope he made the call.

Ramiya answered the phone. "Is you, boy? What you doing up so early?"

"I wake up fore-day morning and couldn't drop back."

"What! Nikki crossed she legs on you?" said she and giggled.

"No, Ramiya. Is not that," said Vivion coldly. "Can you get Mother on the line?"

Tones turned equally frosty, Ramiya replied, "If she was here."

"You saying she not there? Right? So when she coming back?"

"How I would know that? I not yuh mother minder."

Vivion sighed. When in her moods, getting information from Ramiya would frustrate water-boarders. "Ramiya," he said, pitching it pleading. "I want to ask she something important. About the peppers. You know anything?"

"About what? Peppers? I look like a farmer? If you have question for yuh mother, you better come by. You know how she is with phone talking. She going be back sooner or later. And bring Nikki with you. I have some coconut buns for she."

Vivion gave up, said, "All right Ramiya. I'll do that. See you then." He closed the cellie, put it on his desk, and shaking an unhappy head, went back outside to worry some more about the peppers.

ooOoo

EXACTLY AS NIKKI HAD ORDERED, the taxi's horn sounded at twelve-thirty. She, looking like a sailor in a white t-shirt with fat light-blue cross stripes over white bell-bottoms that accentuated her long legs and round butt, they promptly left the house.

Out of the fence gate, Nikki went directly to Aaqilah who, in crisp uniform, was standing at the passenger door. "Aaqilah," she said, "this is Mr. Vivion, my husband."

Surprised but slipping in the flow, Vivion said huskily, "Pleased to meet you. I've heard only the best about you," and offered his hand to shake Aaqilah's.

Clearly flustered, the girl automatically wiped her little hand on her clean white shirt, then took Vivion's fingers and shook deliberately, once, twice, before releasing like they were burning. "Pleased to meet you, sir, I'm sure," said she and did a little curtsy.

"Pleasure is all mine," replied Sir Gracious Vivion, glancing a question at Nikki while smiling down at the abashed young woman.

Nikki broke the awkward scene by opening the passenger door and sliding all the way in.

Vivion followed and watched as Aaqilah gently secured his door. Then as she went around the front of the car to the driver's door, he low-voiced to Nikki, "What's up?"

As quick as it was furtive, she said, "Later!"

Mother was on the verandah waiting for them in her rocking chair. She got up to hug Nikki, and Vivion for the first, realized that Mother was a full head and shoulder shorter than his Nikki. Then Ramiya came out and, a cursory wave at Vivion, grabbed Nikki by her elbow and led her into the bungalow.

Vivion looked at his mother and observed, "All of a sudden everybody is best friends around here. Like I is the poor-me-one."

"Now Vivion, stop with that. You just jealous. Nikki is good people."

"So I could get a hug too?" said he, reaching down to embrace his mother.

She allowed a brief hug, pushed him away, saying, "You going break mih ribs, boy. You don't know yuh strength."

Vivion caught an odd scent of her bouquet.

Prompted by it, he began, "Mother, I—"

She cut him off, "I know. But let we go down in the cellar. It private there."

So carrying her thermos of coconut water, and a glass, they went.

Knees higher than his head, he squatted on the floor beside the rocking chair. She sat in her serious-business cellar chair, a straight-backed bentwood piece with cushioned arm-rests and a blue velvet seat. She poured herself a glassful from her thermos, looked demure eyes at him as she sipped, and asked, "So what's so important? The peppers? That's it? What you expected? For me to let them fall on the ground and rotten? No mister man. You should know by now that that is not me. That is not the mother you know."

Chagrined at her jumping into it so directly, Vivion wiped his sweaty hands one in the other. "So you take care of everything?" he asked quietly.

"Well, didn't you expect me to? Didn't you?"

"I suppose so . . . "

"Suppose? You only suppose? You leave a half a ton of ripe peppers on the trees and gone gallivanting? And you only supposing that someone would take care of business? And you don't even tell poor Nikki? How you could be so cold? Is that how I train you to act to a woman? To any woman? Especially a woman who promise she self to you?" Her quiet voice was all at once chiding and skeptical and disappointed.

Vivion, at a loss for what to say, remained silent. Now in addition to his streaming palms, he could feel his neck burning blood red. Knew the pathetic picture he presented. Sought vainly for a comeback, a response equal to the scene. But nothing came. He stood up, took a step towards the open cellar door—

"You going run away from this, too?" said a Mother's sarcasm.

Vivion turned, "No Mother," he said as his eyes filled.

"I just shame and sorry I let you down."

"Is not me you let down, son. Is yuh own self," she said and sighed. Then patted the rocking chair, and said, "Come. Sit yuh self and let we talk. It have enough blame to go around. You don't have to carry all." Her tone was forgiving, placating, gentle. "Lemme tell you something about yuh mother. Is something about you that I realize long after you show you was smart, winning scholarship and thing. Even after you graduate with high honors then start to go wild, even after that. Is true I was vexed, but one time something you say get through to me. You say that you have to have space to dream. Yes! To dream! And that was what I never realize before. You does live with, you does create dreams and enjoy a life inside them. Not everybody could do that. Me. What I could do is make dreams real, actual. Make them see-through solid like yuh Plexiglas walls. Is what I good at. So don't bear no weight from what happen here, okay. Keep in mind that yuh mother practical. Listen and get an idea from how it went . . . "

So obedient like a contrite mollycoddle, he squatted down on the cool cellar floor while she told him how she had managed his unfinished business.

Wasn't much of a task really. She set to it the evening of her visit with Ramiya and Nikki. While Nikki was collecting her equipment and Ramiya inspecting the house, Mother, curious about the state of the pepper project, had made a quick tour that only confirmed worst fears—the vagabond child, unequal to the task of steering it to harbor, had abandoned his charge and jumped ship.

Yet all was not lost. For her the challenge was to move fast and fix, transform the situation into a fair, even a profitable operation. So eight o'clock next morning she took a taxi to Mr. Maharaj's house and hired him to handle the immediate practicals like contracting pickers and packers and transport for five bountiful acres of specialty peppers.

Next move was to get buyers, and that was where Eshu, Lord of Mischief, smiled on a favorite. One of her tenants, Darshan Gupta, who renting Eleven B four years now, is a brown-skinned Hindu about thirty years old. His father had become rich through a heavy equipment business, road building and so on. Darshan marry up an Irish nurse and they have a chubby freckle-faced five-year-old boy. Two weeks earlier when he came by to pay rent, while chatting— Darshan is a talkative fella very impressed with himself—he told Mother about his intention to join partner with an older Afro-Trini fellow from down South who wanted to start a hot sauce business. The fellow, a Mr. Arthur Pembroke, had a nice business plan and a place to set up shop. He even had a dozen family members ready to be full time employees working for promise. All he needed was funding to get all his necessary mechanical equipment.

As boys, Darshan and Arthur Pembroke's son used to play for the same cricket team in San Fernando. Worrell— named after Sir Frankie—was a quality batsman and once he and Darshan made a sixth wicket hundred-and-twenty-six run partnership in a championship final. Although their team lost the game, those heroics forever sealed their personal friendship. So when Worrell mentioned his father's situation to his best buddy, it wasn't long before Darshan had convinced his own father to finance Pembroke's Pepper Sauce to the tune of a quarter million. The sort of backing that builds confidence and eager, interested investors.

After that, as Eshu fixed it, all the co-partners lacked was produce.

So one, two, three, through Darshan, Mother contacted them with her offer of quality ripe peppers fresh off the trees and ready to go.

An opportunity the hot sauce company readily accepted.

Eight days further on they had harvested the bumper crop from the fields. Only peppers left untouched were plants in the nursery, and they were being watered as usual.

When she was done, Vivion at the same time humbled and grateful, couldn't say a word. Just crawled on his knees to her chair and hugged his mother around her waist, awkwardly and carefully and persisting at it until she relaxed and put her hands about his neck, making it comfortable to share of his emotion.

When, still silent, he had returned to his seat on the floor, she declared brightly, "Your girlfriend Nikki. I getting to like her. She have spirit. She really believe black is beautiful. Spunky! Eh-heh, I liking that girl."

Glad, relieved, and justified though he felt, Vivion did not respond, for in his mind he was vaguely cross and scolding, 'Partner, Mother. The word is partner. Nikki's a lot more than a girlfriend!'

So discombobulated was he by the upheaval of events, it was only when in the taxi going back home that he remembered he had not given Mother the news about

Hideo, and in a way, his side of the story.

Still, for no particular reason, the thought shaped his lips to a sardonic smile.

ooOoo

"THE THEME TONIGHT IS COCONUT!" Nikki declared as she went into the kitchen space. Then for the next ten or so minutes the area hissed with the sound of stir-fry and grew redolent with flavors of curry and garlic and cilantro.

In his study, in front the computer, Vivion licked his lips as he glanced at the clock on the screen. He returned to the article he was reading, realized that he was wasting time as already he had forgotten its headline. He closed the screen and pushed the machine to the back of the desk, actions automatic, unconscious he was making room for anticipated dishes. Then his impatient belly growled and sent him seeking.

He put his chin on Nikki's head, leaned his body along her backsides and asked through her hair, "Need help?"

"You could take in bowls, plates, spoons and forks two-by-two like Noah would. We eating at the big table until yuh friend gone. We have to—"

"We don't have to practice that!" Vivion protested.

"Well, mih darling. I don't mind in the least if you don't mind getting food stains on yuh papers and that fancy cedar desk."

"Hey," compromised Vivion instantly, "so we eat out here. At least the table closer to the kitchen now that I so hungry and every second counting."

"Stop being a spoil child," said Nikki and chuckled. "You eating in less than two minutes. And you eating nice."

Vivion hefted her round buttocks in his big hands, said, "With melons like these, forever and ever tasty."

Nikki twisted herself away. "You better leave me alone," she said, "before that's all you get to eat."

Vivion ran away mock howling. "Is not me, your Honor," he cried, "I does only eat stews and roasts and ting. Cooked animal. Nothing living."

Five minutes later they were busily downing a meal of warm coconut bread with dasheen bhagii for dip and land crabs stewed in coconut milk flavored with Cuban thyme, hot curry, and shadom beni.

Plus other unspoken delights for desert.

*   *   *

When asked, Nikki chose not to accompany Vivion to meet Hideo. "He's your friend, after all," said she, "me there would be a distraction. I'll stay home and prepare a little something for when all-you come back," she reasoned as he called for transport.

So said, so done. Vivion went alone. Aaqilah, looking sharp as usual in her uniform, drove.

The airline being government-owned and operated Trini-style, they got to Piarco half hour before the flight was due. That was more to get convenient parking rather than meeting an on-time arrival.

The flight came in only forty minutes late. Immigration and Customs took thirty-five more and at eight fifteen a broadly smiling Hideo Arata walked through the sliding airport gates free of officialdom, except for its indelible 'Checked T&T' stamps on his two suitcases.

Vivion welcomed him to Trinidad, shook his hand, took the larger suitcase and led him to the transport. Aaqilah was there ready with the trunk popped. "Hello, Mr. Arata," she greeted, "I hope you have a great time in your stay here."

Impressed by the nice touch, Vivion loaded the bags realizing that Nikki's arrangements were more detailed than he ever expected. He and Hideo got into the back seat and Aaqilah glided them off to the palace.

Nikki had drawn the frilly white curtains around the living room and Vivion's study, the front rooms of the house. So when they stepped through the fence gate, the soft light through the tall and wide Plexiglas windows and walls was a luminous beacon. As Vivion punched in the password, Hideo said, "Very nice. Like a Chinese paper lantern. White. Yes! Very impressive. Already I like it."

"Wait till you see details in daylight," crowed Vivion, pleased as he was proud.

He slid the door open and they entered the living-room area suffused right then with the delicious aromas of freshly cooked food.

Then slippers slapping the rubberized tiles, arms wide and reaching, Nikki rushed over from the kitchen area. "Hideo Arata-san," she said with a laugh, "welcome to our house. Consider it your home." Then, just a mite taller than him, she hugged Hideo.

As she did, he sent Vivion a quick surprised glance, and when released, blushing red as a Five-Pot pepper, he recovered to say, "Thank you Lady Vivion," looking bewildered but happily so, and grinning as he exaggerated at a Japanese bow.

All which tickled Nikki to no end. She clapped hands and hopped and laughed out loud. All of it natural and sensual and merry. "Lady Vivion!" she all but screamed. "Oh no! Oh my! Too much! No, to you I'm only Nikki-san!"

Only then did Vivion realize he had never mentioned her to Hideo.

All moot, as Nikki with her exuberance had set a jolly mood.

After a while of polite chatting, Vivion showed Hideo his room on the top floor at the back of the house, the bedroom adjacent to Nikki's work room. In the morning he'd awake to views from two vantages: one of the creek and the pepper fields; the other of the high woods through which the creek passed, and two bamboo stools that lined its banks.

As Vivion left, he winked at Hideo, waggled a forefinger and said, "Nikki made something special for you. She plating in ten."

"Awesome!" said Hideo.

The prepared menu was shark's roe gently fried in sweet

butter; well-done salmon fork-shredded and seasoned with lime juice and cilantro; slices of avocado and ripe mango Julie. These fillers, with a dribble of homemade pepper sauce, were meant to be tucked into the pockets of hand-sized yeasted roti.

Vivion and Hideo dug in right way. Nikki said she wasn't hungry, sat and watched with an appreciative smile. Off and on, to assist the performance, she went to the fridge to bring coconut water, fresh cow's milk with a dash of bitters. The men acknowledged her service with grunts and nods.

It could be that Hideo was unduly polite or very hungry; he had two well-filled roti.

Vivion had no such excuses for his unexpected self-indulgence. He put away three.

At the end of it all, after discreet belches and their pardons with respectful looks, the gourmands agreed to an under-appreciated word as they declared the after-flight snack was 'outstandingly delicious.'

After Hideo had said his 'good nights' and went up the incline to his bedroom, Nikki, in Vivion's study, caught the giggles.

"What? Tell me," said Vivion.

She didn't but continued her bubbly good cheer.

"Come on, Nikki," mumbled a sleepy Vivion, "let me in."

She rolled across the big bed, put her head on his broad chest and whispered, "That snack just now. Today I cobble up the recipe from a Thai and a Japanese menu I look up on the Web. Ent that a riot?"

No answer. Vivion had dropped off.

He was yanked out of a deep sleep by a worry of how to pass on news of the harvested peppers to Hideo. A guy so genuine and open. A guy who so obviously liked Nikki and her cooking. A guy who had put solid trust in so slippery hands as Vivion's. After a bit of restless tossing, for fear of waking Nikki and in an effort to fall back off, he tried deep breathing in a regular pattern.

It wasn't working though. So he carefully rolled off the other side of the bed, sneaked out of his study. He went to the back bedroom with it's view of vague tree-shaped silhouettes of darkness set upon a background blackness that was enhanced by a brilliant, starry sky.

He propped himself on pillows, contemplating the night and didn't know when he fell asleep.

To those curious about the subject, a lot's being said on the Web about sleep being not only the absolute sustainer and restorer, but also the most extraordinarily reliable problem solver. Seems sleep does knit up much more than Care's raveled sleeves. Nothing scientific, but from personal experience, purely anecdotal evidence, Vivion knew this theory was based in truth. He was living proof.

Awaking at dawn Saturday morning, he was light-hearted as a sun beam bouncing off iridescent butterflies. Not a worry on his mind, for it had come to him how to handle the Hideo no-pepper news—he'd tell him the truth and blame it all on Mother!

A hot shower left him full of zest, so he went to his bed

and roused Nikki to impress her. Sometime later he put on
an old-timers' CD, and while she made an early breakfast,
sang along softly with Lord Kitchener, dancing and wining
before, beside, and behind his sweetheart while the master
calypsonian lusted lyrically after Audrey's amazing Sugar
Bum-Bum.

When he came down just before ten o'clock, Hideo
seemed subdued. He wanted coffee for breakfast, but
neither Nikki or Vivion being coffee drinkers, accepted a
brew of homemade cocoa grated into boiling coconut milk,
and slightly sweetened with raw honey from the hives.

Delighted with the taste, two hot cupfuls returned his
good humor somewhat. And as it turned out, maybe his
resolve.

Done with breakfast and ready with his Mother's fault
pitch, Vivion led them through the back door, his heading
the depleted pepper plants. Three steps on, Hideo touched
his arm to stop them, and said, "Vivion, my friend, I have
something, er, to say."

"What's that?"

"It is about business. The business that brought us
together. Our pepper business."

"Yeah," encouraged Vivion.

"There has been a development. I mean, for me. My
part of our contract."

"Contract? Hideo, we don't have a contract. Not yet."

Hideo nodded in his vigorous manner, "Yes. That's it.
You and I, we don't have a contract. So I made contract
with the farmer in Antigua. Mr. Taylor Jackson of Jack's

Pepper Farm. An honorable man. He will supply me a
variety of hot peppers like Moruga Red, Peter Pepper, Seven
Pot, at very, very good price. I made the deal. We signed
contract. I am sorry for this disappoint—"

"No way!" said Vivion smoothly. "Congrats, mih man. I
don't mind at all. Anyhow, I mostly wanted to show you
how I live. Man, I just happy you took the time to come
visit my house, you know. But look how it getting hot
already, maybe we skip the complete plantation tour, eh?"
he laughed hearty, clapped Hideo on his shoulder, "Well, at
least cut out the unimportant part. Let's walk this way and
I'll show you what I mean." And with a swiftly adjusted
itinerary, Vivion switched onto a grassy path that led
towards the nursery.

Basic and functional, Vivion's nursery is a sturdy sixty-
foot by thirty-foot structure with an arched roof. First time
seen, Nikki thought it was a beige colored Muslim wedding-
tent. It's enclosed by a double layer—single on the roof—of
lightweight porous plastic mesh attached to a frame of
reinforced steel poles planted deep. The ventilation pores of
the mesh are the size of pinheads and are meant to keep out
even the smallest flying insects while allowing passage of air,
light, and rainy-day mists when, with floating drifts and
blurred outlines, the ambience inside can be surreal.

Other accoutrement are an active bee hive that's
changed weekly, and an automatic sprinkler that gives
seedlings and plants a fine spraying once every half hour—a
period that can be adjusted.

Vivion was showing off his experimental trays—all ten

of his current cross pollination tests. Hottest peppers lined up on left side of the nursery, moderating peppers on the other. With plants flowering, trays could be wheeled together and isolated by mesh curtains hung down from the ceiling. All ears, Hideo asked, "Is this why seedlings and mature plants are here in same shed?"

"Well, half and half. I only isolate when particular plants start flowering. But I plant seeds from ripe peppers almost every full moon. So I have a constant rotation going. Next season I'll try planting every dark moon. I want to see if the moonlight has a noticeable effect on anything."

"Very nice. Efficient. And with every day a summer's day you can experiment year round."

"True dat, Bro. True dat. You take what Nature handing out."

"In my home we have very fertile volcanic soil—"

Vivion cut in, "—then you could always build a nice greenhouse."

Hideo shot him a skeptical look, said, "And keep it warm and sunny all year round, right? Just like here?" His tone was flat.

"Nah, man. I only joking. That wasn't—"

Just then came Nikki's yell from the house: "Vivion! Phone. Is from New York on Magic Jack!"

"I'll be right back. Look around. Check out the systems. Take your time," said Vivion and left to take the call.

Returned short minutes later he found Hideo red-eyed and scarlet faced, frantically washing out his mouth at the plant-water faucet—the untreated, stored rain water from the ground tank.

Vivion guessed but asked anyhow, "What happen?"

Without stopping sloshing his mouth, Hideo pointed to a tray of mature plants on the left—ripe yellow peppers showing prettily in between dark green leaves—same Moruga Scorpion, but the deceptive yellow variety which was as fiery hot as any, and of which Hideo had had a nibble, probably of a vein.

"Oh, man!" exclaimed Vivion in sympathetic tones and quickly led Hideo to the kitchen. He poured a tall glass of cold cow's milk, said, "Sip slowly. Slosh it around yuh mouth as long as possible before you swallow."

Tears streaming down his cheeks, Hideo nodded and followed instructions. He sipped and sloshed like a penitent zealot.

Sympathetic eyes on him Vivion shook his head slowly. He had never before seen the effect of undiluted Moruga Yellow on a fellow human being.

That afternoon they visited the Bungalow so Mother could meet Hideo. Vivion told the pepper tasting story, and couldn't stop smiling as he did. Although the burn had been long gone, the three women were all tut-tuts and solicitous to the extreme. Mother recalled a Shango remedy that requires bushes hard to come by. Ramiya left the verandah to go brew up a special cure involving coconut water and papaya, and probably brandy.

Although somehow established as the villain of the piece, Vivion couldn't help being amused at their fussing.

Meanwhile focus of all this attention, Hideo Arata-san

never stopped grinning.

Then Nikki said, "I have something to show you," and took him down to the cellar. She put on the light and undraped a stunning portrait of Andaluza. Eyes defiant in a beautiful youthful face. A face of fearless determination. Right away Vivion could divine it was a version of his mother he had until now missed knowing.

"Whoa! That is fine, very fine. Outstanding! Is amazing how you could do that! Girl, you just awesome!" was some of what Vivion said of the impressive portrait. Then, the practice now grown easily on him, he hugged Nikki. Kissed and cuddled, then kissed some more as her bouquet bloomed ripe and right and ready. So they cuddled and fondled each other like impatient teenagers and made promises for later on fulfillment.

Eventually they returned upstairs and had a pleasant afternoon lime with the others until Nikki reminded that Aaqilah, in minutes, was due at five.

When the car-horn tooted, the trio said sayonaras and scooted.

Next morning, Sunday at nine o'clock, Aaqilah driving, they set off for La Brea to see its tar pits and mud volcanoes.

On the way, Hideo began explaining that the term La Brea tar pit was as redundant as saying Sahara desert. In dogmatic manner, he stated, "La Brea in Spanish means 'the tar'. In Arabic, Sahara means 'desert' . . . "

Vivion tuned him out. For no reason at all he was in a funk. Body lethargic, his mind strayed as the blurred world outside flashed by.

He blinked alert when Aaqilah said, "I going try beating the heavy traffic. I know a short cut through this cocoa plantation coming up."

Vivion said, "Sure" and she turned off onto a wide and quite serviceable gravel road. A mile or so on, after taking it slow across an old concrete bridge, they came upon a copse of trees with ripe cocoa pods. So they stopped and Vivion introduced Hideo to the unique sweetness and slippery feel of ripe, raw cocoa seeds.

Hideo took many pictures of the fruits growing straight out the stem.

While they were at this, Aaqilah had drifted away to investigate a buzzing sound. Then they heard her low, excited call, "Come quick, quick, but walk soft and quiet!"

She had found the source of the odd buzz—the busy wings of a determined wolf wasp in to-the-death contest with a fat, hairy tarantula. It was an entertaining and exciting half-hour before the victor flew off with the paralyzed prize—in the flesh of which it will lay its eggs.

Hideo had a blast; he must have taken a hundred photos.

Back en route to the pitch lake, they learned from disgruntled passersby that with the hot sun and all, the melting roadway had been deemed unsafe for vehicular traffic. So it was turn around and head back for the palace, and Hideo never getting to see those tremendous six-inch tall belching mud volcanoes.

Caught up in reviewing photos of the thrilling Wasp vs. Arachnid epic, he didn't seem to mind so much.

Next day, Monday, the six dry weeks of *petite carême* ended abruptly as torrents began pouring at dawn and never let up.

Hideo borrowed Nikki's computer, remained upstairs and caught up with his e-world.

Vivion and Nikki messed around in the study until late morning, then had brunch at midday, took a plate up to Hideo, who was napping. Then they went upstairs to the roof and settled themselves cozy to take in the stormy weather from under the waterproofed Plexiglas canopy.

Reclined in lounging chairs, they read and chatted for a while, then watched and listened to endless rain coming down, and windmill vanes whirling electricity into invisible storage batteries, and rainwater sloshing and rushing along the four-foot-wide reinforced plastic eaves to a tank on the ground.

Then around four-ish, somewhat stunned by Nature's violent extravagances, they went down to cook up a memorable departure dinner for Hideo Arata-san, their first-as-a-couple guest.

The menu:

Salad: thinly sliced, raw bamboo heart, flavored with sour cream, capers, sweet red and white onions, and a squeeze of fresh lime juice.

Entre: cow-foot soup pressure-cooked with secret ingredients that may include salt, shadom beni, garlic, cloves, carrots, chives, and what-have-you. When the combined flavors smell satisfactorily mouth-watering, cornmeal dumplings and eddoes and a whole, unbroken coffee pepper are added until the soup is thick with confident promises of sated appetites. On a side dish are fresh-baked coconut buns with which diners can wipe clean their plates and bowls.

Condiments: Mother's coffee-pepper sauce, mustard, raw butter, grated cheese.

Dessert: Ripe mango Julie, star apple, seedless guava, plumped raisins.

Drinks: Milk, coconut water, orange juice, brandy, Old Oak rum.

Hideo's flight was Tuesday morning eight o'clock. He had to be at Piarco at 6.30. No problem at all. Vivion as company, Aaqilah drove them there. They said 'Goodbyes' at the Departures gate; Vivion stooping to share a brief hug with Hideo, Aaqilah giving him her two-stroke diplomat's handshake. Then Vivion passed Hideo his second bag and they waved him through Security, watched him join a short queue to the ticket counter.

All as per routine.

On Thursday Vivion got an email stating Hideo had arrived home. A special instruction that piqued his curiosity was: "Tell Mother, thanks, and assure her that everything worked out as she suggested."

Good excuse for a ride to the Bungalow, he called up to Nikki after phoning for Aaqilah. "Let's go by Mother."

"Sure," said the sugarplum.

Then last minute, the car tooting outside, she changed her mind. "Boy," she explained, "I just can't leave this idea, you know," while staring at a mounted canvas that showed a single diagonal black line.

So Vivion went alone, and arrived, dismissed Aaqilah as he decided he'd meander his way back home. He relayed the message and asked Mother, "What's that about?"

She chuckled and said, "Well, that boy braver than you would expect, *oui*. All he needed was an idea to spur 'im on. So that's what I give 'im. I show 'im how if you sprinkle the seeds in the bottom of he jacket and pants and shirt pockets—"

"Mother!" Vivion interrupted, "You not telling me that you . . . "

She put her hand up and stopped him. "The boy wanted some coffee pepper seeds," she said with force, wagging her forefinger up at his face. "He want to make a high bred tree. He say you want to do the same thing too. So I tell him I have plenty coffee pepper seeds and I could give him some. So then he start a-hemming and a-hawing about how he going to take them home. About how Customs might prevent them from entering the country and all a' that. I mean to say! What harm some pepper seed could do? Well, pepper seed small. In a pocket crease they almost invisible. So I put the two ideas together and show 'im how to get some seeds home." As she finished, she rubbed her hands in each other and smirked, "As you see, it wasn't that hard."

Smile wide as a piano, Vivion clapped his hands and said, "Mother, you the best. So now you is corrupter-in-chief, too? Oh Lordy! You make a crook out of Hideo Arata, the most honest fella I ever met."

Her pleasure manifest, Mother rolled her eyes and

assumed her haughty, eyebrow-raised, you-may-genuflect look.

Instead, Vivion exclaimed, "Hail to thee! Yo! Mama-san!" performed a curt Japanese style bow, then made gangsta signs with his long fingers.

Mother almost choked flushed-face trying to suppress her laughter.

ooOoo

SUNDAY DAWNED SUNLESS and with a steady, misty drizzle. But it was windless and warm and pleasant and Nikki wanted to walk. Happy to accommodate, Vivion threw on a cotton sweater and went along. They crossed the rude plank bridge and took a track alongside the creek that led into wild-woods on the uncultivated section of the property. After a while she stopped them under a laden Tonka bean tree, hugged herself on him and said, "Viv, this smell, this Tonka bean fragrance, it does make me think of you."

"So from now this tree is mih new best friend forever," said he.

"I not joking, though. Hear this," she murmured and sighed a heavy one, "every day for the first three days after you went, it rained. I mean bucket-a-drop, Noah-get-ready rain. To me, is as if even the sky crying that you gone. So first day, second day, I walking the house like in a cage. I can't do nothing. I looking at a canvas, it remaining blank. I just wasting time. When third day wake up pouring, I decide I not taking it any more. I tie up mih hair, throw on yuh hooded poncho. This same yellow one. And I march outside like a soldier. By the time I reach the bridge mih sneakers going squish, squish, they full of water. But it ent so bad. I could take it. Anyhow, as if the rain get more vex for that, it start storming and pelting down harder, hitting at me. But it can't wet Nikki. Yellow is mih plastic shield. So under the hood, hiding mih face, yuh girl smiling. But then I think of lightning and figure I should show some respect. So I get off the track and come to shelter right here under these branches. Well, boy, with the wet in the air the whole place heavy with Tonka bean fragrance, and all at once it give me an idea about you. Is how you could love a fragrance. Wrap up yuh self in it. Carry it everywhere with you. But you can't hold it or tie it down. You can't capture it with paint. You can't own it. And easy so, that is how I get over missing you."

Vivion tightened his hug as a tear formed and filled and spilled. He sniffed snot up his nostrils, said, "Listen, sweet—"

"No," she cut him off, "don't say anything. I don't mind you going off to deal with yuh jumbies. Really, I don't mind. Is who you is. Is the you that I love."

Through the wet plastic, Vivion massaged his passion all over her back. "Nikki, you—"

She cut him short again, "I thought I tell you not to talk. Anyhow mih darling, what you think about fatherhood and so on?"

Somewhat relieved at the change of subject, Vivion shrugged as he answered, "It cool, I guess. If you have a good father."

"What about if *you* is the father?"

And right off, he caught on that she was saying she was pregnant and his heart raced and drummed a crescendo of elation. Hands strong on her shoulders, he held her off him, searching her face as he said, "Wow! You sure?"

Eyes glistening, she smiled up at him and nodded, "Sure, I'm sure."

His next feeling was triumph that he could now know and equal Spoon's experience. Then plain delight making him once again wet-eyed, he said, "Thank you, sweetheart. I'll be a great father. Don't you ever doubt that. Sweetheart, you make me so complete."

She said nothing, just hugged herself on him, tight, fierce.

A stretch of loving time sauntered by before he disturbed the spell to ask, "You tell Mother?"

Her head shook No! against his chest. Then a little afterwards she cleared her throat and mumbled, "But I think she knows."

"Then I bet is Ramiya who tell she. Taino have animal nose."

"No bets from me, partner. Them two does share everything."

Vivion nodded agreement, hugged his lady around her waist, and started them back to his palace. "It getting damp," he said.

As they crossed the bridge, Nikki said, "I thought you would know."

"How so?"

"Well, you and yuh sharp nose!"

"All I have to say is that since I come back yuh bouquet

get so comfy and warm. I figure it was stronger love from missing the sweet man. Yu'know how they say, absence make the heart grow fonder. Only with you is the scent get stronger," said he and giggled.

Nikki let him feel a strong, fond elbow in the lower ribs.

ooOoo

TEN O'CLOCK IN THE MORNING, bathroom, kitchen, and mundane necessities duly attended to, they were back in the study lolling on the king-size bed when suddenly Nikki got off at the foot and stood before the tall mirror there. She hugged the light blue dressing gown tight around her belly, turned sideways left then sideways right and asked, "Darling, you think I showing yet?"

Vivion fresh-roused, rolled over and assessed her with a lazy eye, mumbled, "Nah!"

Nikki sucked irritation through her teeth, "But Vivion," she said patiently, "you not even looking at me. I's four months plus and mih belly only looking like I overeat. I want the truth. But you can't tell with just a glance. You have to look at me serious." She started the sideways twisting again, this time with hard eyes beamed on his face.

Vivion made much of clearing his throat and drawing himself up while at no time shifting eyes from her body as he jammed his back against the headboard. He cleared his throat again, shook his head and voiced extra low and gravelly, "Nah, man!"

At which Nikki cracked up. She threw herself onto the bed beside him and pillowing her head on his naked thighs, cackled, "That's all you have to say? Nah man! Man! I's a man? Eh? That's the best from yuh long, red, sleepy head."

"Nah, girl," said Vivion in a lighter, smiley voice, "Is how you just slip into mih psychic zone. I was there halfway dozing and it come to mind that maybe is time I go check out yuh parents. You know. Meet them formal. Do and say the right things. And then you jump off the bed and ask if you showing. You can't beat that, right. The karma. The coincidence. So as far as I see it, we just have to go through. Like Mother would say, We have to obey the choice of Eshu, God of Crossroads!"

"Well, beyond all yuh African obeah, I like that idea in truth. While in Buccoo those couple weeks ago, I text Mammy and tell she how I having a good time and all that. Trying to make she feel better 'bout we situation, and from what Andaluza saying, maybe she getting there. Still, I know Mammy would never mention anything I say to Babu. So most likely he really don't know nothing about how I doing." Her voice went ragged for the nonce, then continued, "Boy! Father or not, that man not knowing me at all. It must be hurting him deep. So maybe is time we break the ice."

"Hold on, girl-friend. I think yuh Babu know you well enough, yu'know. I mean you grow up right there in front him. Li'l girl running 'bout naked in the yard. He must've noticed—" But by then he had to forcefully protect himself from a pillow being well-swung.

The women made the visit an occasion. They had presents to take the Grant-Ali's—more fairly, Elizabeth Grant-Ali. Andaluza had a jar of cured pepper-flavored guava jelly, four years old. Ramiya had a recipe for fried cassava cakes. Nikki had a special surprise—a charcoal portrait caught from a shot sneaked with her smart phone.

So everything had to be set up right. First was the date: Nikki, mindful of her father's habits and responsibilities, ruled out Friday (preparation for prayers), Saturday (Mosque duties), and Sunday (visits from sycophant neighbors and needful sundry). Her mother Elizabeth tutored children on Wednesdays, so it was out. Andaluza, for business reasons, scratched Monday and Tuesday. Ramiya was indifferent. Once she had time to do her baking, for her any day was a good day.

So mid-afternoon on Thursday a week later was made D-date.

Passive as salvage, Vivion went along.

The casually dressed trio sat in the back—Mother middling under her broad-brimmed hat. Vivion stretched out in the front passenger seat, and Aaqilah driving, they headed for Torracilla Estate. Today Aaqilah wore a black cap that Vivion thought made her look servile, a cliché of a capped chauffer. Bothered by the scene she might present to the Grant-Ali's, he reached over, touched her shoulder, startling her, "Aaqilah," he said, "you mind doing me a favor?"

"Favor? Sure, sir."

"Would you lose the cap?"

"Lose the cap?" said Aaqilah.

"Yeah," said Vivion, and he gestured to his head. "You look so much better without it."

Aaqilah shot him a doubtful glance. "You want me take off the cap? But is the uniform . . . "

Vivion shrugged, "But I is the customer. And you know what they say, Customer always—"

Aaqilah cut in, "—right. So all right Mr. Vivion, here goes the cap." She took it off and put it on the seat beside her.

With the arrangement that she'd be back at five, she got them into the gated community at three o'clock of a breezy, sun-splashed afternoon. Banks of swift-moving white clouds kept the heat at bay, made the sparsely wooded area cool. A scent of cedar blossoms in the air made it pleasant. Elizabeth greeted them at the front gate, led them through a well-kept lawn to the front terrace and into the grand ranch-style house. Into a spacious living room where, with determined arms folded across his heaving chest, Mr. Osman Ali stood in command.

To greetings from Andaluza and Ramiya Mr. Ali nodded curtly, all the while never stop staring at Vivion and Nikki— a darling who at her man's side stood like a stalwart.

Elizabeth stepped up to Vivion, stuck out her hand to be grasped and said, "I'm Elizabeth, Shanika's mother, of course." Her bright smile reflexive, she held onto Vivion's hand, pulled him towards her husband and said, "And this is Mr. Ali, her father, of course." She grinned nice teeth again.

Mr. Ali looked up at Vivion with a cold eye and nodded. Just once.

In his best, most charming tones and manner, Vivion said, "So pleased, Mr. Ali. Been looking forward to meeting you."

"Well, well," said Mr. Ali.

Interpreting the clandestine squeeze of his damp left hand as encouragement, Vivion said, "Nikki tells me the greatest stories about you."

"Nikki? Who's Nikki?" said Mr. Ali, looking about the airy room as if for a fluttering butterfly.

Right then Elizabeth invited, "Ah! Why don't we continue in the kitchen, eh . . . " somewhat diluting the tension, as everyone released through the dining-room arch and headed towards a big table made of top-smoothed, pinned together, pale oak slabs with varnished, unfinished undersides. Simple looking clever craftsmanship.

Scarcely had the women sat down when, as if by pre-arranged signal, the quartet arose desiring to "see more of the house" and find "where yuh bathrooms be?" and learn that "yuh have a backyard, too?!"

Vivion broke the spell of silence they left, said, "Looks like the ladies leave the fellas to we own devices, eh?"

No response from Mr. Osman Ali. Not even a glance.

Undaunted, the Master of Awkward Moments went on, "Well, since we alone at last, I'm thinking we shouldn't waste the opportunity to clear the—"

"Look here, Mr. Pinheiro," Osman Ali cut in harshly, "you and I don't have anything to clear up. Okay. This situation plain as day. Ask any gossipmonger in the village, ask any muckraker. All a' them know that mih—"

"Hold it right there, Mr. Ali," Vivion interrupted, loud as he stood up all his six-foot-four over the table, "don't say another word you going have to take back. You hearing me?"

"What? What you getting at? Eh! What?" Mr. Ali challenged. Red-eyed. Belligerent.

"What you was about to say," said Vivion as he sat back down, pulled his chair closer to Mr. Ali and continued in a husky, intimate whisper, "listen to me, man. You can't let she know you know this. I give she mih sworn word. So you can't give she any idea. You understand. You just can't. This is between you and me. Okay? Is a matter of principle to her. A modern woman, a sophisticated artist, she is all a' that. You must know what I talking about. You should because she stubborn 'bout she feelings just like she father. But what I want you to know is that we married. So rest yuh head. Quiet and private, first by the J.P in he office, then by the captain of the crossing ship when we did that Tobago week. Was Nikki idea. She romantic that way. She didn't want to disrespect you. I thought you should know this and put yuh mind at ease."

While Vivion spoke, Mr. Ali had slowly turned his slick, reluctant face to square with Vivion's and remained staring at him. His bottom jaw had sagged his mouth to an 'O'. A spot of white spittle had formed at the left corner of his lips. Now he took a deep shuddering breath, forcefully massaged his open mouth with thumb and forefinger. Then hopes and wishes like pictures in his eyes, he grabbed on to Vivion's forearm and said, "You meaning to say. You telling me, that, that all-you married up legal and everything?"

"That's what I telling you, Mr. Ali."

"Well, man, this is the best! The very best news ever. Man, I just want to tell you something." His grip had grown claw-like. Under the shirt's long sleeve Vivion could feel raw bruises forming. "True to mih heart, that was the onliest objection I had to you for mih daughter. I know yuh family is decent, respectable people. I telling you, man to man, it was only that. Now! I just want to assure you that, anything, anyhow I could help out, you don't have to ask. Just call. Okay?"

"Thank you, Mr. Ali. Thank you."

"No problem, boy. And one thing more. Stop that Mr. Ali business. Okay! We is family, both man alike. Call me Osman. I call you Vivion. Okay!" He stuck his hand out and man to man, they shook towards hearty relations.

Later on, back at the palace in the study bed, Vivion related the happening to Nikki. She listened patient to the end, then hugging her belly as she laughed, said, "Vivion, no! You lying to me. You tell him we marry up? And by the captain on the boat to Tobago? A boat captain could do that? Marry people? You couldn't come up with something better?" She was stamping her glee on the bed.

Amused, but shifting a bit so he wouldn't be hit, Vivion said, "I think any ship captain could marry people once you on his vessel," he paused to admonish, "Nikki! Girl, stop laughing so. You going hurt yuh self."

Nikki sat herself up and breathed in several deep,

deliberate breaths. Then, more calmly, asked, "So suppose is a woman captain?" and went into giggles again.

"What you talking about? What go stop she?"

Serious all a-sudden, Nikki turned on her hip, nudged Vivion. "Viv, I have an idea. You know, we could actually get a marriage certificate and fill it out and have it there just in case. And you know I only thinking 'bout who in belly? How you see that?"

"A dummy license? Well, I don't know. It'll have to have the right legal stamps and so forth on it. Not so?"

"So we get them. What ever it needs."

"But who from? I don't want to get Mother into this—"

"Neither me, mister."

"So it come back down to 'who'."

"Listen, darling. I going talk to Janice Peters. She will know somebody. Is what she great at."

"Ah ha! Nikki, you gimme an idea too. You know that pilot friend a' mine . . . "

ooOoo

SHE WAS DOING HER INCLINES, nineteenth lap, up to the back of the house, down to the front. Now in her sixth month and everything excellent, Nikki had come to believe that this daily routine was the reason. Oddly enough, the more muscles-demanding hike up seemed to relax her better, not to mention her sweat glands, and in this rainy season, many a morning it was specially pleasant to refresh her lungs with damp, invigorating air.

Then she'd walk the flat at the back. On clear days, a look right might find action or interest in the forest scenery. Today the light drizzle only made out there hazy.

So then it was to the downward slant, and when she had to be extra careful. Exert patient control. Deliberately slow down. Because in forty or so paces she reaches the bottom, and when she turns the corner and walks the flat front of the house, she could look left through the Plexiglas walls and maybe, see her lover in his study. Get a sneaky voyeur's view.

The greater pull of her belly on the decline, plus the

anticipation of that glance as she passed, always invited this sweet-and-sour excitement.

No luck today, but as she turned the corner to the back flat, he was at the door waiting. He did that sometimes. Nikki stopped and stepped in place when she got to him.

"I was thinking—" he started and paused.

"Was it good for you?" panted Nikki with mock concern.

Vivion chuckled "sniff, sniff" through his nostrils, then said, "*Sí, sí, Señorita. Delicioso*, though not as nectar sweet as thee. But really, I was thinking about a name."

"Sports, politics, crime? Gimme a better clue."

"No, not that. I mean a name for the popo."

"Oh, Vivion! Why you didn't say so?"

"Duh! What did I just say?"

"You know what I mean."

"So you have one?"

"Yup."

"What it is?"

"It private."

Vivion exaggerated a look-around, asserted, "We private."

Nikki stopped marching, sighed and leaned against the banister. "I think I better finish. I can't walk and talk no more." She gave him a determined look, turned into the house, went into the bathroom, slid the door shut.

When Vivion heard the shower turn on, he ambled into her work room, sat on her high stool and spent time looking around at the stacks of canvases strewn about.

Minutes later, fluffy in a light blue bathrobe, hair

disappeared in a white towel, her fresh, smooth face shining, Nikki came in and was careful as she sat herself in a straight-backed chair. Then she announced cheerfully, "Now about this matter of a name!"

Vivion had to laugh. She could be so unexpected. "What is the name? That is the question," he said.

"Well, darling. This is how I see it. If is a girl, you name she. If is a boy, I do the naming. So I picked boy names."

"Already? You have names already?"

"Yup!"

"And you not telling me."

"Nope!"

Vivion did a three-sixty spin around on the seat of the high stool. Returned face to face, he looked at his lover and began nodding as if he understood why her huge grin was so, so triumphant. "Well, I suppose I should concentrate on girl names, eh."

"That seems like a great tactic, or approach, or strategy," said Nikki.

"You want to know the boy names I had?"

"No, *Le Monsieur* Napoleon! Is not my business. I not interested. So on another matter altogether, what we eating on this blessed day? Boy, these days I not so hungry, yu'know. I can't be eating enough." Then opening the robe to display her watermelon belly, she asked, "Viv, you think I putting on weight enough?"

"Oh, you fine, girl. Is yuh height that hiding the weight," Vivion reassured. Then did not understand why his lover abruptly stood up, cast him a dubious look and went stiff-necked into her bedroom.

* * *

They made the top floor theirs. As it was to be a home delivery and Nikki being due any time now, with the help of the three grandmothers, they had done all that was necessary. The doctor, who preferred to be called Mrs. Jones, had visited and given her blessings about the preparations. The only bother was Vivion—he was being anxious. Nikki's every sigh was ominous. A belch, a grimace was menace disguised. So much so, being practical, these days she mostly stayed in her rooms. Furthermore, the late part of her pregnancy had opened a window to novel images, and she was capturing their essences one every two, three weeks. For her these last months had been a marvelous time and having decided on the names Percival (of King Arthur's Round Table) and Ahmed (in respect to her father) she was happy as a lark.

So, unwilling to let her normal pregnancy discomforts provoke her man's caring concern, she isolated herself.

ooOoo

THEY WERE ON THE WAY UP to the back flat. Vivion was trying to convince Nikki that she needn't do another ten laps. "Suppose you strain something, eh?"

"That's a silly idea. You trying to say I weak? You ever think what native women used to do and some still going through to deliver? You have any idea?"

Maybe her belly, these last few weeks Vivion found Nikki to be easily irritated, shrill, and impatient. In fact he was certain it was her babying belly. He said, "Well, you have a point there. Since you start getting close I been reading up about it—" He bared a Dracula grin and added, "—especially 'Do-it-Yourself' methods." Then he glared at her and laughed "Ha-Ha-Ha-Ha!" like Vincent Price in 'Thriller'.

They walked across the back flat and started down towards the front flat.

As they turned and passed the study Nikki looked in and Surprise! Surprise! there stood Andaluza looking out at them smiling as if she'd found the key to happiness.

That was the end of the exercising.

Nikki went up to her rooms. Vivion went through the front door and greeted Mother. "How's it going, Grandmama?"

"And don't you think I don't like the sound a' that!" she said and continued, "So why you have the poor girl climbing around the house like that? You don't think carrying a belly ent hard work enough?"

"Mother, mother. Wait, I—"

"I don't want to hear a word. Why you don't go out for a walk or something? Go stroll through yuh estate and think of how yuh mother make you so lucky!"

He went.

In straight chairs on the back flat, looking out at an unremarkable view, both sipping coconut water, Andaluza turned to Nikki and asked, "So how it going, child?"

"Is not so bad you know. Last week, off and on I was getting some cramps, but they don't frighten me no more."

"Nah! You shouldn't be. You ent the preemie type. Not that I's any expert from the only one I—" She looked away quickly, uncomfortable. All at once wet-eyed.

"Andaluza!" cried Nikki. "Don't do that to me. Okay. Don't you! I won't stand for it!"

But Andaluza turned streaming eyes back on Nikki, said with a voice that shuddered through heavy breaths, "But you don't know, child. You just don't know how it hard to make a child in shame. To raise it. You can't ask, you can't tell nobody. You can't figure it out for yuh self. You down to one person who'd be there anyhow. Child! You could never understand how I envy you. How I wish to Lord

Eshu I coulda been you!" She covered her face with her hands and sobbed.

Time after, Nikki pulled her up from the chair, "Let we go in the bedroom. I don't want Vivion find we here in this state."

Obedient as a robot, Andaluza took direction, followed into the room, but as Nikki was closing the door, said, "Where Vivion does keep he brandy? I feeling like a sip."

"In the freezer section. He like it cold. If you going down there, you could bring a glass of milk for me? "

"Of course, my child. And thanks. That was a really heavy burden." Andaluza said softly as she went.

They sat side by side on stools at her work-table. As Nikki accepted her milk, she looked askance at the quarter-filled tall glass of brandy Andaluza held.

"You not even seeing this. Okay," said the older woman. "Don't worry. Is not a bad habit or anything. And don't put it on Ramiya. Is just off and on. Special times . . . you know."

"You talking to moi, Missus Pinheiro?" said Nikki. "With mih belly big so, I gone blind as a bat. How I go see anything over this bump?"

"Child, you too full a' foolishness," said Andaluza, smiling as she sipped her cold brandy. Then in a lowered, intimate voice, said, "Listen close, Nikki. I going tell you something I never tell anybody before. Not even Ramiya know the whole score. And you should keep it that way. But! You making he baby so that qualify you. Is about

Vivion father. He was cousin to the brother of a classmate I meet in a graduates reunion school party. He was from New York, on vacation in Trinidad, and had to return home in a week—" she closed her eyes as if to refresh the vision and a wistful smile came to her face as she rhapsodized, "—Child, you shoulda see 'im. Tall and slim-thick, could dance like a star-boy. Does hold you light like he letting go. But he not. Then he have hair carrot-color and curly and you just know it soft like a new cotton ball. And he eyes does change color so! Sometimes they soft grey. Sometimes they greenish blue. You just can't stop looking at them. He say is how light hitting them. But girl, that boy was pretty in truth. I mean really handsome pretty. And with mischief in 'im like a funny house-monkey. And laugh! He could have me laughing so. I really, really did like that boy, you know." Her voice now was quiet, musing.

Nikki took the pause to ask, "Andaluza, you keep calling him 'him'. What! He don't have a name?"

Andaluza jutted up her chin and turned away as if she had not heard. She hugged her shoulders and rocked side to side to some pleasant personal rhythm. Then with a shy simper, she said, "I used to only call 'im 'K'."

Nikki gave her a raised eyebrows 'pull-the-other-one' look and said, "Madam, is your story, okay. So go on."

"Well, as somebody I know does say. Long story short, seven days was enough for young Andaluza to fall mad in love with K. So as with everything else, she confessed to and consulted with soul sister, Ramiya.

"Naturally, mih issue was, What to do while I keep mih pride and purity?

"Well in the end it work out fine. I mean it was hard work for both a' we. But I manage my side. Fact, I was so good that after K went home unsatisfied in one way, he was totally fulfilled in another, and we keep up a passionate correspondence. Every month at least one letter, sometimes two, coming and going as close to a year is flashing by. Then, in September he write asking me to come up and join 'im as he date to he college graduation. College graduation! I mean he even had he parents and sisters support that the invitation was proper and decent. Imagine. I still have that letter. Not a wrinkle on it. Keep it like new.

"Remember! This was going on towards the all-a'-we-is-one Eighties. I was turning twenty. So what else I going do?

"Yuh girl went to New York, spend four glorious weeks and come back home with a belly. Me and Ramiya keep it between we self until a month from delivery. Then we band the belly, make it look smaller, and take a flight to New York. Why? Because it big and anonymous. And K was from there. So with mih soul sister caring for me, we stay at a Howard Johnson's in upper Manhattan until right on time, three weeks later I deliver in Harlem hospital emergency. Both a' we agree that the boy born with star shine on 'im. I say is Eshu favor. 'Cause after hearing details of mih situation, the obstetric Nurse Williams feel sorry for me and advise that in filling out the forms, I should use true personal information like age and such. Then she would provide a real American address and other necessary particulars because any false statements woulda spoil the validity of the birth certificate.

"That good woman name was Vivian Myrtle Williams.

And that's why mih boy is Vivion. The middle initial K is all that I take from he father."

ooOoo

As if the baby was waiting for them, Nikki went into labor half an hour after Mother and Ramiya arrived.

At once taking command, Mother ordered Vivion to call Mrs. Ali while Ramiya called Mrs. Jones, the obstetrician. Twenty minutes later both women were in the house.

The four of them remained with Nikki in the top-floor rooms, comforting her during labor pains that were going on about three hours now. Last time Vivion tried to check, maybe hearing him jogging up the incline, Mother met him at the back door, turned him around with advice, "Boy, you going only nervous she. As a first-timer, already she feel she not doing it right. But in truth she okay. She young and strong. The doctor say everything proceeding fine. So you just don't worry."

Vivion cast her a baffled wide-eyed look which she shrewdly parried by gazing out at the commonplace scenery. Shaking a perplexed head, muttering his argument to himself, he took the incline back down. "What's this not-to-worry she talking about? What she getting at? What I suppose to do? Mih woman in serious distress. All that pain, suppose she get too weak to push out the baby? Suppose something else happen? Something unexpected? What I supposed to do then? Not to worry?"

He hung his broody head and went into the study to sit and stare out unseeing at the cloudy, indifferent afternoon.

Two hours later, he made egg sandwiches and tiptoed up the incline hoping—under the pretence of delivering snacks and cool, coconut water—to sneak into Nikki's room and see what was happening. He turned the corner and met Ramiya leaning against the banister tippling from a tall glass.

"Vivion, you is such a nice boy," she exclaimed. "Look at me, forgetting I was peckish. Brandy does do that to you. But let me take that in—"she took the tray from him—"Luz and Elizabeth going appreciate this. And Mrs. Jones, too. And Oh! Nikki doing fine. Contractions coming every ten, five minutes. So is any time now. You just go back in yuh study and relax. Don't worry!" Ramiya spoke kindly but firmly and with a gentle hold at his elbow, guided him back the way he had come.

Defeated, unresisting, Vivion went.

As happened before, the idea arrived while he sought solace from anxiety through wetness. This was trusted therapy—soaking in the shallows, basking under a warm shower, even doing dishes as he now was making busy with. Always conservative regarding water use, his practice was to pull the faucet's lever shut each time he put a cleaned dish in the draining tray, then hit the lever back to 'open' as he rinsed another. But this afternoon, every time he did, something unspecific quibbled, and remained a persistent bother until he put his mind to reasoning out the matter.

He let the warm stream wash over his hands while he started a debate between he and his nagging self:

Vivion: Is this about the faucet lever? How I handling it? Too forceful, maybe?

Quibbler: No, not in this instance.

Vivion: So is it the faucet, or the lever itself?

Quibbler: Maybe.

Vivion: Hmmnn. Then, is it about efficiency?

Quibbler: At, or, of what?

Vivion: The excess, perhaps? The sudden rushing flow? The immediate gushing?

Quibbler: You close.

Vivion: Yeah! I's the man! So then, you thinking about a way to slow that rush? Eh? To stop wasting the precious gush?

Quibbler: For that, all to do is return to old style circular faucets you twist and turn anticlockwise to open and increase the volume poured? What about doing that?

Vivion: Well, I'll go along with that and raise you another. What about we combine the two ideas. Gradual increase of volume with increasing physical effort to make it happen? What about that?

Quibbler: Well, tell. You know we'll go along if it workable.

Vivion: So what about making the increase action an incremental zigzag instead of a circle?

Quibbler: ! ! !

*   *   *

Here we leave Vivion K Pinheiro in inventive euphoria. A place of mind where he's most comfortable. Where all his prospects are promising and every limitless horizon beckons. So praying that Lord Eshu protects him, we send him off.

P.S.   It's a boy! A few minutes ago Percival Ahmed Pinheiro weighed in at nine pounds, fourteen ounces. A ruddy brown, healthy fella twenty-three inches long with gray-green eyes. The scant hair on his scalp is jet black, soft, and curly.

Glossary of Trinidadian terms:

Aloo Choka: Herb-flavored mashed potato example of tasty Indo-Trinidadian cuisine

Base: Bass note steel-drum of Trinidadian Steel Orchestras

Bobol: Corruption; Nepotism; etc.

Callaloo: A unique vegetarian side dish made from dasheen leaves and varied personal favorite ingredients like coconut milk. Land crab and callaloo is a delicious staple.

Doughla: Mixed-race person, one of whose parents is an Indian

Doux-Doux: A sweet, sweet mango variety; a term of endearment

Lime: A hangout; to loiter; to socialize; the occasion itself

Maccoe: A busy-body; a Nosey Parker; a peeper/voyeur

Maccomere: A woman's close female friend

Mamaguy: To make a fool of someone; to deceive; to swindle

Petite carême: A short (4 – 6 weeks) dry season within the rainy (5 – 6 months) season

Phulourie: A fried curry and cumin flavored flour balls, very tasty

Picong: an exchange of japes and jibes that are usually

funny, but can be painful

Pulling bull: Slang term for working as a part-time chauffeur

Tabança: A severe depression; the blues from missing, or losing a lover

Vi-que-vi: Devil-may-care; irresponsible, though can be charming

Wine/Wining: a Trinidadian dance that involves seductively wiggling one's hips in rhythm

More books from Harvard Square Editions:

CPSIA information can be obtained at www.ICGtesting.com
Printed in the USA
LVOW10s1618080515

437779LV00005B/427/P